MAYBE THIS TIME

PORT SIMMS
BOOK TWO

ANN ROTH

Cover art by Dar Albert at Wicked Smart Designs

Published by Oliver-Heber Books

0 9 8 7 6 5 4 3 2 1

CHAPTER 1

January third and a Friday to boot, Rose Shafer woke up with a smile on her face. Today was her twenty-sixth birthday! She wondered what Peter would get her this year. They'd been married almost twenty months, with more downs than ups, but Peter made up for that by paying for shopping sprees and trips to spas wherever she chose to visit. Last year's birthday present had been amazing—a herringbone gold-chain necklace with a sparkling diamond front-and-center that rivaled her four-carat engagement ring. The delicate gold wedding band was pretty, too.

No matter what, he always took care of her. She no longer worried about how to pay the bills. An added benefit of marrying an older man. She was perfectly capable of taking care of herself. But Peter had told her she no longer needed to work, icing on the cake of their relationship.

Physically, he wasn't great in bed and not the best at expressing his emotions. And lately, he'd been gone more than usual, either putting in grueling hours at the hospital or traveling to various medical conferences. A workaholic and respected surgeon, he'd committed his heart and soul to his work at the Port Simms Hospital. A top-notch hospital, the best in Port Simms.

He'd put in an especially long stint yesterday, leaving before she'd opened her eyes and coming home sometime after she'd fallen asleep late last night. She'd waited up for him, as she had something exciting to say. He was likely still asleep. Knowing him, not for long.

She turned over to wake him with a kiss, a rare occurrence due to the different hours they kept. But no, he was already up and out of bed.

Self-doubt ate at her excitement. Sometimes, she had her doubts about what he did around work when he wasn't home. She supposed it was natural to feel this way. After-all, she was wife number three. A handsome, respected surgeon who'd chosen her, and his charm and attention were irresistible. But now—No, she wasn't going to think about that on her birthday. It was a sure bet he'd make up for the neglect big-time. Who knew what she'd get this year? She couldn't wait to find out.

Maybe he was still here, and she could share her exciting decision before he left. After donning her winter white cashmere robe and soft-soul sheepskin slippers and running a brush through her hair, she headed downstairs to greet him. The thick carpeting muffled any sound.

Their twenty-year-old house had been decorated according to his tastes, with dark oil and watercolor paintings on white walls and lots of antique furniture. Not what she'd have chosen—she preferred warm colors and more modern, comfortable pieces—but this was his house and his money, and she'd grown used to it.

She found him at the kitchen table, inserting a folded piece of paper into an envelope. He looked surprised to see her. "You're up early. I was finishing a note and about to wake you. There's something I need to tell you."

When was the last time he'd planned to wake her before he left? He must have quite a birthday surprise in store this year. She smiled. "Does what you're going to say have anything to do with my birthday present? I have something to tell you, too. My announcement can keep."

"You first," he said, skipping over the part about her birthday. He nodded at the envelope.

She eyed it with excitement. Was he giving her a trip somewhere? "All right, here's my news. I've decided to go back to Simms Bay Community College and finish my degree in interior design! Two in-person classes instead of online that are twice a week. There's also an internship, but I don't know much about that yet. Winter quarter starts this coming Monday."

She'd left the program when Peter had proposed some three years earlier. Totally wrapped up in him and their life together, she'd set her dreams aside and dropped out. Which was okay with him. She'd been wanting to go back for a while now, and had finally taken that step toward her long-held dream. "It's time I finished, and I'm very excited."

No reaction from her husband. She tended to get a little chatty when she was revved up, and he'd always been one to drift off into his own thoughts. But this felt different. A funny feeling settled in the pit of her stomach, so strong, she wrapped her arms around her waist. "I expect what you want to say has something to do with my birthday, right?" she asked hopefully, bringing the subject back to her big day. He didn't appear to have heard the question. What was up with that? "Did you hear me, Peter?"

"I did. I'm leaving."

"Another medical conference? I was hoping we could celebrate together and maybe eat out tonight."

He shook his head. "You misunderstand. I'm leaving *you* and filing for a divorce."

"What?" The stunning news silenced her, although deep down, a part of her had known. The signs had been there for months. The longer and longer hours at the hospital, eating dinner there instead of with her, the extended time periods he spent away from home during medical conferences.

But divorce? She stared mutely at him.

"I've fallen in love," he said.

Ouch, ouch, ouch! She wasn't the brightest bulb in the chandelier, but of his three wives she was definitely the smartest, although her IQ was nothing to write home about. And probably the best looking, if she could be un-modest for a moment. She knew this after checking the exes' social media posts. Must be losing her edge. "Let me guess—she's younger and prettier than me."

Peter shook his head. "He's forty-one, the same age I am."

"He?"

"That's right. Avery is a surgical nurse at UCLA Santa Monica Medical Center. I've accepted a job there and will be moving right away."

Peter was gay? As numb as she was, it made sense and filled in a lot of blanks.

None of her sexual experiences with previous partners had been wonderful, but sex with Peter had ranked at the bottom. An opinion he likely shared, as they hadn't had any in almost a year. She'd begun to doubt herself as a lover, but his explanation proved it wasn't her fault.

Even so, the words, the sudden announcement, cut deep. *Don't cry. Do not,* she counseled herself, but her traitorous eyes filled anyway. Peter was leaving her. She chewed on her thumbnail and she stifled the wail clogging her throat.

He placed his hand, which was warm, over her icy one, and gave a sympathetic squeeze. "I'm sorry, Rose. It was never my plan to hurt you, but after forty-one years, I couldn't live with myself pretending anymore. It feels good to be honest about who I really am." He straightened his shoulders. "I'm a gay man, and proud of it."

In a weird way, she respected him for finally being honest, even if he was abandoning her. She wiped her eyes and sniffled. "Thank you for telling me."

"Of course. My attorney is drawing up the divorce papers now. You'll be served sometime in the next few days."

So sudden. Despite her numbing shock, she recognized that she needed a lawyer of her own. Who knew how she'd pay for that. "Then what?"

"If we both sign the papers and skip any contesting, I believe we can take care of business online. It's the quickest and easiest option. Otherwise, we'll have to go to court. That could take a while."

Take care of business? Such a cold thing to say, when he was ripping the safety net, the security she depended on, out from under her. She wondered who to contact for help. "Can I stay here for a while? You're never at the house much anyway and won't have to see me. I'll sleep in the guest bedroom."

"Sleep wherever you want. I'm driving to Seattle and flying

out tonight." A three-hour drive from the house to SeaTac airport.

"Tonight?" She didn't want to be alone, especially today. Who could she find to celebrate with at this late date? Her sister was out of town, and Pressley and Ragan, her two besties, likely had Friday night plans lined up. "What about my birthday?" she asked, unable to stop herself.

"I'm sure you'll figure something out."

Gee, thanks. "Here's an idea—since you don't have a present for me, how about paying my college tuition," she ventured, out of habit widening her eyes as she always did to get what she wanted. "I have to pay it right away."

"How much is it?"

When she told him, he winced. "That's a lot." She widened her eyes again, and he gave in. "All right, consider that your present. It'd be nice if you stayed here until the house is ready to put on the market. I'll take care of the utilities and throw in grocery money to help you get back on your feet. My contractor estimates he'll finish in six to eight weeks. At that point, you'll have to leave."

"Six to eight weeks? You must want quite a bit done. Wait —you're selling the house?"

"Renovations take time. And yes, as I don't intend to come back here, getting rid of it makes sense."

Décor and dull paint colors aside, she loved the place. "What if I don't want that?"

"It's in my name, Rose. You signed the prenup."

She'd stupidly never considered there would potentially be a day down the road when she'd have to be on her own and take care of herself again. "Yes, I know, but—" Questions crowded her mind, which remarkably seemed to be functioning. She couldn't afford to live alone. Where would she go, and how would she find roommates?

"There are no buts, Rose. My mind is made up. Kenny Martin, the contractor, will be here in a few hours to take any measurements he needs."

"Today? Do you know the man? Can you trust him?"

"I think so. Blake recommended him."

"My brand new brother-in-law?" If Blake knew about the split-up, then so did Rose's sister, Vi. After their wedding last weekend—Vi had learned she was pregnant, an unexpected surprise that seemed to delight them both, and more power to them. Rose looked forward to being an aunt but couldn't imagine having a baby of her own, not after her childhood. It was a wonder Vi embraced the idea, but then, they felt differently about all kinds of things.

Vi and Blake had put together a quick wedding and were currently away on their honeymoon. If they were aware of what Peter had pulled, it was a sure bet Gran and Malcom also knew. Both approaching eighty, they'd married about six months ago and were blissfully happy.

None of them had said a word to Rose. Talk about humiliating. "Am I the only one in the family in the dark?"

"No one knows about this, Rose, except you. I told Blake I wanted to make improvements on the house."

That was something, at least. Blake and her Gran's new husband, Malcom, were savvy businessmen and might be able to recommend a competent lawyer who didn't charge an arm and leg. Although she didn't want to bother Blake. She'd talk to Malcom instead. "You know how little I make at Panache." The boutique where she worked part time once a week, just for something to do. "I don't have much money saved up, and college tuition is due now."

"Yes, you've said that. I've already contacted and hired a moving company to pack up and deliver my things," Peter went on. "I got up hours ago and put green stickers on the art and the rest of what I want in my new home. My clothes are already in boxes."

He'd done all that very quietly, the sneak. He was still talking.

"They'll be here next Friday. Phone numbers, et cetera are listed in the letter." He handed her the envelope.

After sneering at the thing, she stuffed it into a pocket in her robe. "Back to the contractor. Does he know what you want done?"

"I showed him last Tuesday."

He'd actually taken time off from work? Not something he did often. "When I was getting my massage and lunching with Pressley and Ragan?" Her besties. They both worked full-time but had taken a few hours off to get together that day.

He nodded.

"Why didn't you tell me sooner, Peter?"

"You're right, I should've given you advance notice. Too late now."

Would a week or at least a few days have hurt? "What do I do with the things you leave behind?"

"That's up to you."

In other words, he expected her to take care of his castoffs. She wanted to lash out, but what was the point? In her whirling mind, an idea began to take shape, something she wasn't sure she could pull off and wanted to mull over.

"Did you ever love me at all?" she asked, hating the

pathetic, pleading note in her voice. Hating the wimp she was and always had been.

"I loved you as best I could."

The words did nothing to alter the bitter taste of betrayal in her mouth. "I have to admit, for the past year, with you pulling away from me even more than usual, I should've guessed. Are you coming back here again?"

"I don't plan to. I gave notice at the hospital two weeks ago."

Yet another piece of information hidden from her. How many more secrets did he have squirreled away? "This is a big deal, Peter, and completely unfair to spring it on me like this. I can't quite wrap my arms around it."

And yet, she'd intuited that something unpleasant was coming. Too bad she'd refused to believe it. Note to self: trust that funny feeling inside. She could tell he was anxious to get out of there right away. Better share her idea now. "I'm supposed to get rid of the stuff you don't want *and* direct the movers *and* keep an eye on the contractor, all while I'm in school? Those are big, time-consuming jobs. I should get something in return."

"You'll be living here rent free with no household bills, and I'm covering your tuition. That's enough."

"Not for me, it isn't." She'd never been this bold with him or anyone, had no clue where the courage had come from. Desperation, or maybe she'd picked it up from Vi. Her sister had always been outspoken. "I'll be contacting my own lawyer about that."

Peter exhaled loudly. "Go ahead, hire an attorney if you want. If I'm going to pay you, I expect daily text updates in return."

"All right. And *I* expect my payment upfront, including the tuition." They'd always had separate bank accounts, but she knew his balance was much higher than hers. "Check, cash, and/or Venmo are fine." She thought a minute, then pretending she was Vi, named a hefty amount that popped into her head and included more than enough to keep her solvent for a while. The least he could do. *Ha, Peter!* Her boldness made her hands shake, and she hid them in the pockets of her robe.

"That's a lot of money. What if I don't want to pay upfront?"

Birthdays and lavish gifts aside, he kept a tight rein on day-to-day expenditures. Plus, she now knew what a dirty sneak he was. She had no doubt that if he didn't pay upfront, he'd likely renege on the agreed-on amount and give her far less. "Then the deal's off," she said, astounded at her moxie. First time for everything. With nothing to lose, there was no reason not to stand firm. "Maybe I won't stay here, and you'll be in the dark."

Swearing under his breath, he negotiated with her, back and forth, but she stood her ground until he gave in. He gave her cash for half the amount, then Venmoed the balance while she peered over his shoulder and watched him do it.

When he left, she sat down at the kitchen table and cried.

* * *

JUST SHY OF noon that same day, Kenny Martin pulled up to Dr. Shafer's beautiful home. He would've come earlier but had wanted to finish up the bathroom he'd remodeled for an older couple who needed grab bars and a shower floor that wasn't slippery. Work that entailed putting in a new floor, new tile and grouting, installing extra supports on the bars to anchor them, and a fresh coat of paint. A small job, but the pleased couple had paid well and promised to give him a positive review online.

He needed both to help his two-year-old renovation business grow. Also to finance the materials needed for his own home improvements, which needed more time and attention than he could spare but was slowly shaping up. With this job, he stood to make a substantial amount.

The doctor's house was in an upscale area. Built some twenty years earlier, it fit perfectly with the neighborhood, but parts of it needed updating. The doctor wanted to sell it for top dollar and had decided to get the kitchen and bathrooms into tiptop shape, a boon for Kenny. He owed Blake Wanamaker for recommending him.

After leaving the construction firm where he'd worked for several years, he'd started his own company. Blake had been one of his first customers. Completing this job would boost his growing reputation and bring in more business, meaning more money and expanding with a bigger team. The years of schooling and learning how to run his own company were finally paying off. Best of all, the doctor was paying him quite a bit.

The drapes were drawn, but with the doctor gone that came as no surprise. Whistling, he grabbed a kit of measurement tools from the back of his pickup and headed up the front walk. The key was hidden right where the doctor had said, under a fake rock near the front steps. He set the toolkit down and unlocked the door.

He heard the shriek as soon as he opened it. A woman,

pale, who looked like she'd been crying—nose red, eyes puffy, hair hanging limply to her shoulders, yet stunningly beautiful —came at him ominously clasping a brass figurine of some kind in her fist.

Who the heck was she? Struck dumb, he set the kit down and held up both hands, palms up.

"Who are you?" she said.

"Name's Kenny Martin." He reached into his pocket and handed her a card. "Who are you?"

"I'm Rose, Peter's—" she broke off and sniffled. "For now, I'm Peter's wife."

For now? The doctor had never mentioned her. "I didn't expect anyone to be here. Dr. Shafer told me where to find the key."

"Then Peter didn't tell you. Of course he didn't, just assumed I'd roll with whatever he'd planned." She glanced down at her bathrobe and frowned. "I meant to shower and dress, but it slipped my mind."

With the heavy-looking thing clutched in her hand and her face twisted in a mixture of fear and anger, he had no doubt she meant to bash him with it. Treading carefully, he eyed her warily. "You okay, ma'am?"

"Don't call me that—I'm way too young. My name is Rose, and no, I'm not okay, not even a little. Today is my twenty-sixth birthday, and guess what I got from Peter? The news that he's filed for divorce and moving away to be with his new lover. Can you blame me for being upset?"

Kenny heard that loud and clear. "I've been through a divorce myself."

"Is that why your eyes are sad?"

They were? No one had ever mentioned that. Probably

because he felt her pain and sympathized, and for good reason. In his nearly thirty years on the planet, he'd suffered through his share of sorrows and loss. The father who'd left him and his mom around his second birthday, the stepdad who'd moved on after eleven happy years, and his own ill-fated marriage. Not that he regretted the end of the marriage. Getting away from Crystal had been a giant relief.

He mourned the loss of a long-held dream of sharing a life with someone, but had mistakenly chosen the wrong woman. "I don't like thinking about the past." He'd worked hard to put all that behind him. "Happy Birthday."

"Thanks. I wish I felt like celebrating, but I don't. I haven't talked to anyone, not even family, since Peter dropped his bomb hours ago."

Her eyes started to fill and he feared she'd cry, which scared him more than anything. Nothing like a weeping woman to make a man feel helpless. To his relief, she pulled herself together.

"He said you were coming at some point today, but I didn't expect you to unlock the door and let yourself in. I figured you'd at least knock or ring the doorbell."

"If I'd known you were here, I would've."

"Damn you, Peter, for keeping us both in the dark!" Her lip curled at nothing in particular and a bleakness darkened the space around her. Then, seeming to catch herself, she brightened a little. "It's not your fault. Sorry I came at you with this brass angel. I've always hated the thing, but good news, it has a green sticker on the bottom. That means he's keeping it. I hope his boyfriend doesn't mind. As it turns out, Peter's gay."

Each to his own. She'd shared a lot of info that was none of his business. Not wanting to waste time standing there while she ranted when he had measurements to do and supplies to order, Kenny cleared his throat. "I'm here to take measurements and had best get on it."

"Right. I'll stay out of your way. What exactly are you planning to do?"

Her husband hadn't told her that, either? Between that and announcing he wanted a divorce on her birthday, he sounded like a selfish, class-A jerk. Hadn't picked up on that the other day. "I've been hired to update the bathrooms and kitchen plus patch the walls and repaint them—improvements that will increase the sales value of the house."

"As I'll be living here until it goes on the market, please leave at least one bathroom untouched until you finish the others. That way I'll be able to shower, et cetera."

She'd be under foot the entire time? Kenny wasn't at all happy about that.

Almost as if she read his mind, she added, "Don't worry, I won't be around that much. I need to find a steady job and juggle it with college."

Stuff he'd been doing since he was old enough to have a paying job. "You'll be busy, that's for sure. What school?"

"Port Simms Community College. I dropped out when Peter proposed. Dumb move," she muttered. "I still need ten credits to get my degree in interior design."

"That's a good school." He'd gone there himself before getting a degree in construction management at the University of Washington.

"I enjoyed it. I wish I'd finished my degree on time, but I will now. Go ahead and do whatever you're here for. I'll be in the den down the hall."

When he finished several hours later, she was still in the

den with a blank look on her beautiful face and staring into space. Been there, done that. Grief and misery couldn't be hurried, they would take their own time. He poked his head in. "It's a nice day. Why don't I open the drapes to cheer things up?" She nodded and he pulled them open in the den. Much less dreary.

"I'm leaving now," he said. "I won't be back till Monday, but after that I might come on an occasional Saturday."

"Good to know." She resumed staring into space.

"I have several questions," he said.

"Yes?"

"Do you want me to return the key?" A pain, as she might be out when he needed to get in. But if she wanted that, okay.

"Keep it." She stood and put her hands in the pockets of her plush bathrobe. "I'd appreciate a heads-up text when you're on the way over here. You gave me your card, but it'd be easier if we shared contact info on our phones."

Once they did that, he asked the second question. "Okay if we tackle the kitchen and one of the bathrooms first?"

"At the same time?" She wrinkled her nose as if that was a bad idea.

Currently, his permanent team consisted of himself, Augie, a guy he'd hired when he'd first opened the business, and a phone service to wield calls. He also had a list of skilled people he worked with and trusted to call on—tilers, plumbers, electricians and painting pros, all of which he'd need. Finishing as close as he could to eight weeks, max, was important, as Dr. Shafer had offered a bonus if he finished within that time frame. "That's the plan. Unless it's a problem."

"How long will it take to work on both?"

He'd already estimated that. "Several weeks for the kitchen and about the same for the smaller bath upstairs. That will take less time than the master, but the powder room down here should be fairly quick. Of course, it could all change if we run into unforeseen problems." Which was why he'd warned the doctor that doing everything he'd been hired for could take longer. "In all honesty, there'll probably be some. Always are, but my crew works hard and we'll do our best to finish on time."

"No worries from me if you don't. I'm in no rush to leave. Any more questions?"

He nodded. "Which upstairs bathroom do you want me to tackle first?"

"All my stuff is in the master. Please start with the guest bath."

"The master bath last. Okay. What about the kitchen?"

"A few weeks of renovation isn't that long, so whenever. Now I have a question for you. Is Peter paying you directly? Because he didn't say anything to me about it."

He nodded. The doctor had already written a check for a sizeable advance, with a bonus due if he finished in eight weeks or less. "Any other questions?"

"What time are you planning to show up Monday?"

"Around seven-thirty."

"In the morning? So early, but that works out for me. I'll be leaving around eight for class. It doesn't start till nine, but if for some reason I'm not able to pay online, I'll need to do it in person. Between classes and an internship, I'll be out pretty much every day. No idea why I'm telling you this when you're not interested."

As long as she wasn't crying, he didn't mind. "Good to

know your schedule. See you Monday." He extended his arm to shake her hand, something he usually did upon first meeting a customer. She'd been too startled and upset to do it then.

She hesitated as if she didn't want to, then went for it. She had soft, delicate hands, fine-boned, and a direct gaze. Her eyes, no longer red and damp with tears, were an unusual pale green. The seductive, plump, bow-shaped upper lip was tough to ignore.

Well, damn, he was attracted to her. Forget that. Nothing worse than getting tangled up with an unhappy woman and her big problems.

They dropped hands at the same time and each took a few steps back. "I'll let myself out," he said in a gruff voice he didn't recognize.

She walked him to the door anyway, then locked it loudly and firmly the second he stepped outside, as if she couldn't wait for him to go.

CHAPTER 2

Funny, after Kenny left, the house felt sad and empty. Rose was used to being there by herself, which she'd never enjoyed, but this was different. No wonder—her world had been turned upside down. In the few hours he'd been here, they'd spoken to each other all of thirty minutes, but the simple act of him being here doing his thing and tromping around had somehow blunted the silence and loneliness.

That and his eyes. A golden brown, they'd shone with compassion and caring, without a spark of sexual interest. She wasn't used to men shaking hands with her, liked him for treating her as an equal instead of getting flummoxed by her beauty or trying to flirt the way most men did. Not that she didn't soak up the admiration. But today, she'd looked her worst. Still in her bathrobe, no makeup, hair a mess, pathetic and weepy.

His warm hand had all but dwarfed hers, and he'd looked directly into her eyes as if he truly saw her. It was then that she'd noticed his looks. Long eyelashes she envied, a handsome face with a classic Greek nose, and a sensual mouth. He was built, too, muscled with broad shoulders and a flat belly—or so it seemed in his long-sleeve, flannel shirt and loose jeans.

Surprising that she'd taken all that in when she'd been angry and numb, but now that he was gone she realized he was super attractive. Even if she didn't really care.

It was getting late, and her phone had been unusually silent. And on her birthday. She pulled it from her pocket and frowned at the screen. No wonder—she'd left it on Do Not Disturb, had been too distracted to notice until now. As soon as she switched the phone back to regular mode, calls and message notifications appeared. Lots of them.

She read Vi's first, a birthday greeting filled with love and good wishes and an invitation to dinner on her, sisters only invited. A tradition since the tough days when they barely had enough to buy a muffin and split it, let alone a meal. A similar Happy Birthday message from Gran and Malcom, and one each from Pressley and Ragan. Since meeting in an interior design class at the community college, their friendship had thrived and they'd grown super close.

They'd been through broken hearts, weddings, triumphs, and failures, and she counted them as almost family. They all were sure to flip out when she told them about Peter. She dreaded that, but they needed to know.

She started with Vi. Telling her on the phone would've been nice, but the Virgin Islands were three hours ahead, and for all she knew the newlyweds had gone to bed early, being honeymooners and all. Sharing the bad news in a voice message would be tacky. Either way, the news was sure to put a damper on their fun time. In the end, she sent a brief text about the split between her and Peter, asking Vi not to call her back and they'd talk when she got home.

That done, she phoned Gran, who was more like a mother than Angela, her hairdresser mom who lived in Houston and had never cared much about her or her sister. Vi, being five years older, had acted as a surrogate mom for most of their childhood, even after their gran had moved in. Although Gran had taken some of the load off. Their father, who lived in Hawaii with his longtime girlfriend, was also mostly out of the picture.

"There you are," Gran answered. "When I couldn't reach you and didn't hear back, I was beginning to worry. I assumed Peter had taken you someplace special. Happy Birthday, Rose!"

There went the tears, flooding her eyes. *Hold it together,* she silently ordered herself. "Thanks, Gran, but sadly, this birthday is anything but happy."

"What's wrong, honey?" she asked, her concerned tone spiking a pitiful sob from Rose.

Fighting for control and losing, she poured out the story. "Now you know," she finished with a pause to blow her nose.

"I'm gobsmacked and so sorry. I had no idea he was gay." Gran paused. "Know what I think? He wasn't good enough for you."

Gran was sticking up for her, trying to make her feel better. Rose had felt that way, too, only about herself. She had minimal smarts and no college degree, in other words, little to offer besides her looks.Which was probably why Peter had married her, she now realized. "Thanks for saying that, Gran. I need a lawyer. Will you ask Malcom for the name of someone I can afford?"

"He's out right now, but I'll have him get back to you as soon as he's home. Better yet, why don't you come to dinner at the 709 and he'll tell you in person?" The retirement home where Gran and Malcom lived and where they'd met. "Or we can go out."

The thought of their sympathy oozing over her during a meal wasn't at all appealing. "Thanks, but I'm not in the mood. Maybe another time."

"All right. Let me know if you change your mind. Expect a call from Malcom within the hour."

Last on the list, Rose texted Ragan and Pressley an SOS and requested a conference call ASAP. They were each at their respective workplaces, but they knew an SOS was serious. Besides, being a Friday afternoon things were likely winding down. Somehow, they managed to take a break at the same time and phone her. Once they were both on the line, the gory details poured out. They insisted on coming over that evening, both to commiserate and to celebrate her birthday, even if she didn't want to.

She didn't, and yet she did. "I'm a mess, and I'll be terrible company," she said. "But if you want to come, I won't stop you. Give me a few hours, okay?" She wanted to deposit the cash Peter had paid her into her bank, mainly because putting it there felt safer than keeping it in her wallet. Later tonight, she'd use some of what he'd Venmoed her to pay her tuition online.

Knowing her friends and family had her back made her feel better, enough that she took a shower, tidied up the kitchen, and finished the leftovers from the previous night's dinner, her first and only meal of the day.

* * *

Rose's posse arrived shortly after six. Port Simms being in the Pacific Northwest, darkness had fallen a few hours before. They brought treats and set several bags down on the antique table in the entry. One of the few antiques in the house she liked, which Peter had, of course, stickered.

As soon as they slipped out of their winter coats, they put their arms around her for a trio hug. Of course, she cried. Again. "I'm so tired of these tears," she said, swiping angrily at them.

"After the shock you suffered this morning?" Ragan said, tucking her chin-length auburn hair behind her ears. She was married. "If Marcus had done that to me, I'd be on the floor and probably plotting his demise." Her lips quirked. "Chocolate always helps, and we brought tons. Let's open the treats."

They headed into the kitchen. Moments later, they set a chocolate layer cake in front of her and stuck two candles, a two and a six into it, plus an extra to grow on.

Touched, Rose patted the area over her heart. "So pretty. It's from Melissa Ann's, huh?"

Pressley nodded, her gorgeous blonde hair swaying gently. "Four layers of heaven in the mouth. Nothing but the best bakery in town for our bestie. Make a wish and blow out the candles."

Rose was quiet a moment, figuring out what to wish for. Then she blew out the flames.

"Tell us what you wished," Ragan urged.

"Isn't that a no-no for birthday wishes made over blowing out a candle? Never mind—I want to share this. I'm going back to school. I wished for a career in interior design after I graduate." She wasn't sure she'd get it, but putting it out there couldn't hurt.

Ragan smiled. "That's great. You have real talent, and you shouldn't let it go to waste."

"What she said," Pressley agreed.

Rose didn't see herself as talented, but if they did she'd take it. "I'll be living here until the house goes on the market in a few months and suffering through the renovation mess." She wrinkled her nose. "I made a deal with Peter to keep an eye on the guy he hired for the job and send daily updates about progress made and setbacks. That'll be a pain. On the positive side, I forced him to pay me upfront for my services. *And* I negotiated for a decent amount of money. Me, of all people. Can you believe it?" For the first time that day, she smiled.

"You usually aren't so outspoken," Pressley said. "That must've felt really good. Kudos."

"Thanks. I only wish you could've heard me. I was badass."

Both friends laughed. "Must've shocked him something awful," Regan said.

Rose grinned again. "It was the first time ever I stood up to him. He didn't like that at all."

"About time you grew a pair," Pressley teased. "We all know how picky Peter can be with his money. How did you do it?"

"Simple—I threatened to move out and leave the house in the contractor's hands. He about had a fit, but I held firm."

Ragan beamed at her. "Smart and savvy, Rose. I'm really impressed."

"I'm not smart or savvy except about fashion and design, and we're all aware of that. I did it out of desperation."

"You really know how to land on your feet."

"When you grow up the way I did, you have to." One of the handful of skills from childhood she'd learned.

"That's an important tool, but don't you dare short-change yourself on your other cool traits. Insisting Peter pay you in the first place and holding firm when you were barely functioning proves how smart and tough you are."

Pressley nodded.

Rose soaked up the praise. "Tell that to whoever hires me. I need a job that allows me to go to school and do the internship."

"My internship turned into a permanent position," Pressley said. "My dream job." A colorist, she'd interned at a commercial design company and was much in demand by corporations wanting fresh color schemes for building interiors. "Of course, I waited to intern until I was finished with the coursework and available to work full-time. That way, I made enough to pay the bills."

"Hopefully, you'll be paired with a company that pays you for your time, like we both were," Pressley said, holding up crossed fingers. "Of course, my story is different from Ragan's. I worked part-time at the place where I interned. As it turned out, I wasn't so good at selling tile or window dressing. But working there helped me figure out what I wanted." She had a great job at a commercial real estate company where she decorated office buildings for various clients. "I'm saying that even if you do get paid, you don't have to stay with the company where you intern. I'm very happy at Custom Design."

"I envy you both. I'll get there, too, I hope. According to the community college's description of the internship, it'll be part-time at a company sanctioned by the school. Right now, I need a job that pays enough to cover rent and other bills. A roommate or two would help with housing expenses. But even if I had the money to live by myself, I've never tried it, and I'm not sure I want to."

"I like living alone," Pressley said. "I clean the house when I'm in the mood and don't have to answer to anyone. How many credits do you need to graduate?"

"Ten. I'm going to register later tonight and plan to sign up for the last two courses of the program. In one quarter—ten weeks—I'll finish. Having been through it yourself, Ragan, you know juggling classes and an internship can be stressful. Maybe you were smart to get the classes out of the way first, Pressley. But I want to get all of it done at the same time. School starts Monday. I'm lucky they're letting me in at the last minute. Who knows where I'll end up doing the internship."

"Google and find something in the field that interests you." Ragan paused. "But with you coming in at the last minute, that might be difficult. I'm sure your instructor will help with that."

"Too bad my employment record is so spotty." With Peter footing the bills, Rose had worked part time since the wedding and had moved from job to job on a whim until settling in one afternoon a week at a store she really liked. "I'm still working at Panache—their clothes are so cute. Over the past few months, I managed to put away my paychecks, small as they were, so I have a little saved up. The money Peter paid me fattened my bank account, but it won't be long before I need more. I guess I can ask Panache for more hours, but who knows if they'll want me. Oh, and Malcom gave me the name and number of a good lawyer. I'll be phoning him in the morning."

"Good for you." Pressley looked thoughtful. "Do you have a resumé ready for any job interviews?"

Rose shook her head and sighed. "I'll add that to my to-do list."

"So, who's doing the renovations?" Pressley asked. "Maybe I know them."

"His name is Kenny Martin. I met him this morning, a few hours after Peter walked out." Remembering, Rose cringed. "I was a teary mess and still in my robe and slippers. I'd barely combed my hair and hadn't brushed my teeth since the night before. I'm sure I looked like a crazy woman to him." She paused. "He's a big man with muscles to spare and eyelashes I covet—quite the hottie."

Pressley's eyes widened. "You noticed that when you were so upset?"

"Not at first. When I settled down and stopped tearing up, it was hard not to."

Both women leaned forward. "Is he married?" Ragan asked.

Rose shrugged. "My brother-in-law recommended him— he built a shed for Blake and did a great job. That's the sum total of my knowledge about him except that he's divorced."

"He told you that?"

The oh, so interested looks on their faces...Rose eyed them. "I think he said it because I was really upset." Embarrassing, for sure. "He said he knew how I felt, because he'd been through a divorce himself." His unforgettable eyes had looked straight into hers with such understanding. Why did she keep thinking about that?

"How old is he?" Pressley asked.

"Hard to tell. Late twenties, I'd guess."

Her friends nodded. "I'm sure he forgave you for pouring out your problems," Ragan said.

"At first, he was shocked that I was there. Peter hadn't mentioned me, the rat, and Kenny assumed the house would be empty." Her anger flared, but why get stirred up again? "Oh, and Peter hired a moving company to pick up everything that has a green sticker on it. He did most of the stickering while I was sleeping. He must've been up most of the night. The movers will be here next week, Friday, I think. I'm supposed to take care of whatever's left of the stuff he doesn't want."

"What does that mean?"

"I can dispose of it any way I choose."

"That could work out in your favor." Ragan tapped a finger to her lips. "I hope he leaves some of the antiques behind. They're worth a lot. You'll make a mint off them, unless he expects you to give him the money."

"I'll be keeping that, thank you very much. I'll contact antique dealers soon."

"They'll probably want photos to get an idea what you have," Regan said, "and maybe will ask to see the real thing. I know because I helped my mom sell some of the pieces my grandma left her."

A few moments of chatter about antiques went on before Pressley spoke. "Did you love Peter? At first, you seemed to, but you haven't said much about him for the longest time, except to talk about how you felt like you were living alone. He sure was gone a lot."

This was true. "Did I love him?" Rose mused. "That's a

good question. He was charismatic and seemed to adore me at first. And I thought I adored him. And his lifestyle was pretty enticing, and I wanted the financial security Vi and I never had growing up, the shallow part of me has to admit. Then, once the glam and glitter of the wedding faded and life settled down, reality wiped the stars from my eyes.

"The man was at the hospital twelve hours a day and always going to medical conferences. He usually stayed at those a few days before and after. It didn't take me long to realize he was buying me off with gifts so I wouldn't make a fuss about him always being away. It worked, too, but coming home from trips to find him gone? I didn't like that. I'm not like you, Pressley. Going to bed and waking up alone night after night gets old fast. It's been lonely.

"Any love I felt for him wore off a while ago. The entire time we were together, we were never that close. And the sex was pretty bad." Both friends gave her sympathetic looks. "Wait'll I tell you the kicker. Peter left because he's fallen in love with someone else. A man his own age."

Jaws dropped. "Get out!" Ragan said. "'Not that there's anything wrong with that,'" to quote Seinfeld. I'm surprised, that's all."

"I was shocked, too, although I guessed he was seeing someone else. And hey, it's better than leaving me for a younger woman. Helps keep my pride intact. He stated loud and clear that he finally feels like himself. But I feel like I've been hit by a truck."

"Oh, sweetie," Ragan said. "No wonder the sex was bad. Consider yourself lucky to be rid of him."

"I second that." Pressley shook her head. "I wonder why he didn't come out a long time ago."

"He didn't say." Rose shared something else she'd thought about earlier that day. "I'll bet he's been sleeping with guys the whole time we were married."

"Better get yourself tested for STDs."

In all the turmoil, she hadn't thought about that. "Another thing to add to my to-do list. I'll go in tomorrow."

Her friends stayed another hour, talking, nibbling at the cake, and sipping wine. By the time they left, she felt much better. Could be the chocolate and wine, but mostly, she'd needed their love and support.

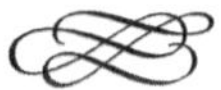

CHAPTER 3

That same evening, Kenny got together with his best buddy, Milo Gifford, aka Buddha, the nickname his parents had dubbed him due to his chubbiness as a baby. The chubby phase ended, but the nickname stuck. Kenny met him at Come on In, a favorite of theirs. Great burgers and sides, and a decent selection of on-tap beer or the bottled stuff to choose from. In the past, they'd hung out a couple times a month, but since Buddha had gotten married a few years earlier, they didn't see each other that much.

The blue collar diner was noisy tonight, and once they'd ordered, Kenny raised his voice so Buddha could hear. "How are things at Gifford Building Supplies?" The family-owned business where Buddha worked and would someday run. Kenny had worked there, too, during high school, where he'd discovered a love for building things. By then, they'd known each other and become best buddies.

"Life is terrific." Buddha grinned. "Kendra and I got some great news yesterday. We're having a baby."

"No kidding. Congrats." Kenny tipped his pint glass and saluted his friend. He envied the guy, wanted a family of his own. Always had, from the time he'd been a little kid watching his mom struggle as a single mother raising him. He'd dreamed of a real family with a father and at least one sibling. Some years later, when he'd been on the cusp of eleven, she'd married Mitchell, a great guy. Later that same year, she'd given birth to Abe, the brother Kenny had always wanted. At last, a real family—for the ten years it lasted. Then his mom and stepdad had divorced, partly due to money problems.

"What's Kendra's due date?"

"Late July."

"A summer baby. Boy or girl?"

"We won't know for a few months. We're fine with either one."

"I'll bet your parents are happy."

"They sure are. Their first grandchild. They send their love."

It'd been a while since Kenny had been in touch with them. "Send mine back. I've always been grateful for your father," he said during the meal. "For giving me a job and teaching me how to make a budget and open a savings account. Without him, I never would've saved enough to buy that old Chevy Impala or financed my two years at the community college. I couldn't have gone to the University of Washington, either." He'd passed on what he'd learned to Abe, now a freshman at the same university.

"I remember that old car." Buddha shook his head and grinned. "It was almost ready for the junk pile, but we had some good times in it. I got a lot of action in the back seat."

"The good ol' days," Kenny agreed. "The front wasn't bad, either."

While they dug in, Kenny thought about Brandy, his mom. She was still single and still bad with money. Her job at the dry cleaner where she'd worked forever paid enough for rent, but she often struggled with the bills. Which reminded him. Her birthday was exactly ten days from today. He intended to be there and hoped Abe would be, too. For his brother, that meant driving home from college. He wouldn't want to miss school, but no problem. Brandy wouldn't mind if they celebrated over the weekend instead of on the actual day.

"What's up with you?" Buddha asked. "How's your house remodel going, and how's business?"

"The house is coming along slowly. I work on it evenings and Sundays. Saturdays, too, when I can. I finally smartened up and hired Augie to help. I now have insulation throughout the house and energy-efficient windows in every room. The place feels nice and snug. I expect to see a big difference in the heat and AC bills."

"Nice. What's next?"

"Augie and I started tearing out the wall between my bedroom and the adjacent room to make a decent-size master bedroom. That's about half done. It'll be a while before we finish—I just got a renovation job from a bigwig surgeon over at the hospital, or he was. He's relocating to California and has already left town. He hired me to renovate the kitchen and three bathrooms and paint the interior."

"Where's the house?" When Kenny told him, his buddy whistled. "Rich part of town. That'll be a boost for your business. Get him to give you a review."

"I will. He gave me a key to come and go, and I went over

there this afternoon to measure for supplies. I assumed I'd be walking into an empty house, but no, his wife was there. He never mentioned her."

"What? That's weird."

"Yep, and she was real upset. A few hours before I showed up, the doctor had asked for a divorce and told her he was leaving town and selling the house. No advance notice at all." Kenny couldn't get over that. "Brutal, huh?"

Buddha scratched the back of his neck. "It's harsh, all right. Wonder why he did it like that?"

"She didn't say."

"Maybe she cheated on him. Or she's unhinged, like Crystal."

Kenny winced at the thought. "She didn't seem that way, was more in shock. I asked her a few questions about the house, spent an hour or so taking measurements, and split. Which reminds me, after I left, I called Gifford's and ordered some of the supplies I'll need. I'll pick everything up around six Monday morning."

"That's why we open early."

"Always happy that you do. Will I see you there?"

"Nah. I've been coming in around nine. What's going to happen to the soon-to-be-ex-wife, whatever her name is?"

"Rose." Kenny couldn't forget the feel of her delicate hand in his. Or the flash of attraction he'd felt when their gazes had met over that hand shake, douche that he was. He'd been hired to do a job, nothing more. She didn't seem to feel anything at all for him. With the shock she'd been through, he'd have wondered if she had.

To his relief, the feeling had quickly faded. Yeah, he felt for her and her rough circumstances, but that was it. He really needed to start dating. "Today was her birthday. What a crappy time to find out her husband wants a divorce and is leaving town." Kenny shook his head. "She's going to stay in the house and keep an eye on things till the work is done and the place is ready to go on the market. She's also going back to school at Simms Community College. Monday, I think. Something about finishing her degree. That's the sum total of what I know."

"A fair amount for the short time you were there."

Kenny shrugged. "She was upset, I was there, and she needed to let it out."

Buddha looked at him with a sage expression. "Don't do it, Kenny."

"Do what?"

"I know the signs. That poor-unhappy-woman face tells me you want to rescue her. That never works, and you know it. Crystal had big problems you couldn't fix. You ended up getting hurt."

He'd liked that she'd depended on him and wanted his help when she needed to make a decision. He was flattered that she looked up to him. "She really wanted to get married, so we did." Remembering what'd followed, he swallowed. "I wish we'd slowed down."

Buddha nodded. "No one thought you two were a good idea, but you'd made up your mind and nothing was going to change it."

Biggest mistake Kenny had ever made. As the honeymoon phase of their marriage quickly faded, Crystal became demanding and volatile. The hair-trigger nasty temper she'd hidden often erupted for no known reason. Living with her had been hell. A scant year after the wedding, the marriage had ended. "My head's on straight now. How about two pieces of pecan pie on me, to celebrate the pregnancy? "

"Can't turn that down."

Over dessert, Buddha picked up the conversation where they'd left off. "Be careful with the doctor's wife, okay? Save yourself a world of hurt."

"I don't intend to get involved with her. But shock, I'm ready to get back on the horse, meet someone and settle down. Heck, I'm almost thirty. It's time. The woman I choose won't be messed up like Rose. She needs time to come to grips about losing her husband. If she's smart, she'll find a good therapist to help."

"She's gonna live in the house, though."

"Like it or not. I'll see her and ask her questions when something comes up. Other than that, I plan to steer clear."

"Good plan."

Not long after that, they finished the meal and parted ways.

* * *

Saturday morning, Rose heard from Vi. "You poor sweetie," her sister soothed, reminding her of when they were kids and she needed comforting. Their parents had partied and fought and partied some more in their spare time, leaving Rose and her to fend for themselves. A mere five years her senior, Vi had been stuck mothering her for most of her childhood. They were still close, but Rose no longer needed her sister to play mother.

"Yesterday was the worst," she said, "but I'm managing."

"Tell me what happened."

Rose repeated the story she'd told her friends and Gran, also sharing the deal she'd forged with Peter to oversee things for a hefty fee. The more she thought about that, the prouder she was of herself for sticking to her guns instead of striving to please him the way she always had.

"Good for you," Vi praised. "What a bum he turned out to be."

"You can say that again. Living with a man who's gone most of the time and is pretty much shut down emotionally has been frustrating. It was nice, though, not having to worry about juggling the bills. Plus, he paid for my clothes and beauty treatments without question and showered me with beautiful jewelry." She glanced at her left hand before remembering she'd taken off the engagement and wedding rings last night to the applause of her friends. "The only thing missing was love."

"You can always sell the jewelry and anything you don't want that he left behind."

"For me to clean up. Nice of him to saddle me with that, huh? I'm not ready to part with the jewelry just yet, but if things get really tight, I will. I'll add it to the to-do list. I'm getting an STD test in a little while." Rose glanced at the list. "Also on the list are contacting antique shops around town to find out if there's any interest in the stuff Peter left behind. Oh, and Malcom gave me the name of a good attorney, so that's on my list, too. Although I have no idea if lawyers work on Saturday. Because I signed a prenup, I doubt an attorney will be able to do much for me, but I won't know if I don't try. I need to work on my resumé."

"Look at you, Miss Smart and Practical with your to-do list."

Everyone made lists, but this was the first time she'd written one down. "I learned to put it in writing from the best—you."

"I'm proud of you. Signing up to finish school, too. That's so cool. If you need help with the resumé, let me know." Vi had a high-level job at DD Telecom and knew a lot about that kind of thing.

"I will. I'm excited about school. I'm making myself a hot fudge sundae tonight and streaming a movie."

"Anybody coming over?"

"Just me, and I'm fine with that. No moping allowed."

"You're keeping busy, and that's good."

"I'm used to finding my own entertainment. Peter was gone so much, I had to. I wasn't about to sit around, pouting. Even when he was home he rarely suggested anything fun except a nice dinner on my birthday." A sob escaped from deep in Rose's chest, and she scowled at nothing in particular.

"You okay?"

"No. I'm angry and hurt and wish to God I hadn't signed that prenup. But I will be."

"I have no doubt of that. For a long time now, your relationship with him was rocky and your feelings blew hot and cold. I have to be honest, I always wondered if you loved him."

"Ragan and Pressley asked me the same thing last night. As I explained to them, he was charming at first and I thought I loved him. But when things settled down after the wedding excitement, the warmth faded. Before long, so did my feelings. I guess I never really loved him. I'd probably feel differently if he'd loved me. Maybe."

Having never been with a man who truly loved her, she had no idea. "The way he dumped me on my birthday without any warning or thought about me and how I'd take the news was both disrespectful and hurtful. Right now, if you don't count that teensy sob, I'm in control of myself. Yesterday was a different story. You should've seen me when Kenny came over."

"Kenny? Ah, the contractor Blake hired to build a new shed. I met him briefly once. He seemed nice and he's very good-looking. What did you do when he arrived?"

She didn't comment on Vi's opinion about his looks. Her sister would be all over that, wondering if she'd already moved on. She hadn't, not that fast. "I made a complete fool of myself." Remembering, she cringed. "He stopped by a few hours after Peter left to take measurements for the renovations. I was such a mess that I was still in my pj's and robe. I even cried a little. He looked scared, poor man, and I don't blame him. He's starting the work Monday morning, before I leave for school. Enough about me. How's the honeymoon, and how are you feeling, future mama?"

"We're having a great time in the Virgin Islands. This pregnancy was a big surprise for us all, but I'm almost thirty-one and it's time. We're over the moon about it. You saw me at the wedding. I didn't look pregnant then and still don't. Yet. Except for tender breasts and waistbands that are starting to get snug, I don't feel anything, either. I'm told that won't last long and that morning sickness and maternity clothes are just around the corner. Anyway,"

Ugh on the pregnancy thing. Rose was glad she wasn't pregnant. "I'll bet. Take lots of pictures, okay, and send my love to Blake."

"Will do. Remember, I'm treating you to dinner for your birthday. Just us."

"I'm already looking forward to that. Love you, Vi."

"Love you, too."

As soon as Rose disconnected, she headed for the local clinic to get the STD test. Back home again, she texted her mom about the latest. Then she started on the rest of the to-do list. Having a concrete agenda and checking off items on the list as she got them done helped her make it through the day.

CHAPTER 4

When the alarm went off Monday morning, Rose was already half-awake. She was used to Peter getting up and heading for the hospital while she slept later, so nothing seemed amiss. Then she remembered—he wasn't part of her life anymore. Even after three days apart, it still felt weird. Despite his being away so much during most of their marriage, he'd always been in her thoughts. What to make for dinner, which more often than not she ate by herself, how to please him, where he was, and when he might come home. None of it mattered anymore. Which left her feeling hollow— she'd put his needs first for so long that all the worry and stress seemed natural. Without it, she felt lighter.

For the first time, she realized the burden she'd been carrying since day one of their marriage. No more guessing games or feeling sad or sorry or any of that. Today was the start of winter quarter, something to look forward to. Having paid the tuition bill online soon after her friends had gone home Friday evening meant she didn't have to rush quite so much to get to the bursar's office. She still needed to pick up a list of books and other needed supplies for the two classes, but having over an hour before she had to leave left plenty of time to shower and dress.

As good as she felt about going back to school, a new worry replaced the old one. Despite having more funds in her bank account than she'd ever had, it wouldn't last forever. She wasn't going to spend a penny of the lovely funds on restaurant food. Not until she had a steady source of income. Which meant making herself breakfast and packing something for lunch.

Then she remembered—Kenny would be here in roughly thirty minutes.

With no time to waste, she scrambled out of bed, decided on what to wear—a pair of winter white Alex Mill jeans and a burgundy cashmere turtleneck that made her skin look rosy—and jumped into the shower. She was out again in about five minutes, a record for her. Wouldn't you know, Kenny texted then to let her know he was on his way, just as she'd asked him to. He expected to arrive within the next fifteen minutes.

Yikes. She dressed, made up her face and pulled her almost shoulder-length hair into a high ponytail fast enough to surprise herself. After a look in the mirror and satisfied with the results—not to impress Kenny or her future classmates, simply because looking good made her feel good, she assured herself—she headed downstairs, through the living room, then down the hall past the dining room to the kitchen.

In her opinion, this was the one room Peter had requested for renovations that didn't need much. Maybe a new floor and counters and a different paint, as the off-white color throughout the house made it seem cold and dated. The light fixture wasn't great, either, and the sink and faucet could use an update. But the appliances were top-notch and the cabinets high-end. A few minor touch-ups on the interior shelves would be nice, too.

With any luck, it shouldn't take long to make the changes in there. Which was good, as she'd need access to the stove and oven in order to cook.

The coffee was brewing and she was fixing herself a quick omelet when Kenny let himself in. No time to shed the bib apron she'd donned, and she hurried toward the entry.

"Good morning," he said, wearing a heavy unzipped parka over a faded flannel shirt and jeans.

He was just as good-looking as before—intense golden-brown eyes, thick, dark hair, full lips and the Greek nose. Standing in the entry, he pulled a pair of floor-protector booties over his heavy-duty boots. So did the three twenty- or thirty-something people who'd followed him inside. She'd forgotten about the crew, had assumed he'd arrive alone. She felt oddly disappointed, then decided she preferred the small group to just him.

"Guys, this is Rose," he said. "Meet Griff, Augie, and Nell. They're here to help with the demolition and will be with me during most of the renovations."

"Hi," she said. All three gave solemn nods. Serious types, similar to their boss. Like him, they slipped booties over their work shoes. Thanks to Peter having removed his coats and stowed them in a green-stickered trunk, the closet was half-empty. She gestured at it. "You're welcome to hang your coats in here. Does anyone want coffee? I'm happy to brew a pot for you."

Kenny shook his head. "Maybe for later. Right now, we have work to do. Looks like you're doing some cooking."

"Making breakfast," she said and glanced down at herself. "As you can see by the stains on this apron, I need everything I can to keep my clothes in reasonably clean shape. I'll brew a big pot of coffee. When you want it, help yourselves. I'm about to eat and grab something for lunch before I leave. What time do you expect to finish today?"

"Probably late afternoon. I ordered a dumpster for debris. Okay to put it in the driveway?"

"As long as I have room to get in and out of the garage." She'd try to stay away, then, so as not to bother them.

"You won't get in the way," he said, as if he knew what she'd been thinking. "I'm taking the crew upstairs to show them what we need before we come down again."

"All right. If you leave before I get home this afternoon, please lock up."

The man and his team tromped up the stairs, and Rose sat down to breakfast with a copy of the resumé she'd started working on the day before. Between the footsteps thudding around upstairs and the snippets of conversation drifting down, concentrating wasn't easy. She decided to leave early to pick up the classroom schedule and get the needed books and supplies. She poured herself a coffee in a to-go cup, then started a fresh pot and hung her apron on the hook in the pantry.

It was a decent enough morning, cold and clear after sleeting rain the previous night. Port Simms didn't get much snow, but with the temperature often freezing or below, ice on the roads was possible. Apparently not today, as the streets seemed easy to negotiate. Traffic was mildly busy but not heavy, and she let her thoughts roam, thinking about the disruption in the house. Living with that wouldn't be pleasant, but it was what it was, her new motto as of yesterday.

As she'd expected, she arrived at the community college well ahead of when she needed to be there. In the three-plus years since she'd last been enrolled, nothing much had changed. After checking to ensure she'd paid for two classes, the bursar handed her the schedule, which would've been emailed to her if she'd paid sooner. The classes, worth six credits total, were back-to-back Mondays and Wednesdays, an hour long each, with a fifteen-minute break between. The internship made up the rest of the ten credits needed to graduate. It was scheduled for Tuesdays and Thursdays, six hours per day, for eight weeks. To graduate, she'd need verification of attendance from someone at the company where she interned. She was also responsible for writing a final paper about her experience. That and go to classes, turn in any assignments there, and pass tests. A lot of work sure to take some used to. At least she had Fridays free.

So much for a steady day job. The internships Ragan and Pressley had completed had been important to their careers, and Rose looked forward to the experience. Next stop, the bookstore across what was a grassy area in warmer weather, muddy after the previous evening's rain. This morning, thanks to a concrete walkway, she was spared muddying up her ankle boots. Over the weekend, she'd upgraded an old graphics app, another hit to her bank account, and loaded it into her iPad. Other than a textbook or two, she wouldn't need to buy much else. She hoped.

Due to the cold, the breath puffed from her lips in clouds. It was nice to get inside and warm up a bit while she gathered the reading material and other needed supplies. Fellow students milled around, searching for the textbooks they'd need. To her relief, there were used copies of the two required books, saving her money. She gravitated toward the bulletin board to see what was posted.

How had she forgotten about work-study jobs on campus? She looked through the postings, taking photo copies of positions she might be qualified for. Including the bookstore. Needing to get to class, she didn't have time to apply.

The class size was small—eleven in all, two of them male. Which made sense, considering the enrollees had completed the other classes required to graduate and earn a degree. Rose had worried she'd be the oldest one there, but several seemed around her age. The instructor, who looked to be in her fifties and wore khakis and a pullover, greeted people with a friendly expression. When the chime sounded, indicating the start of class, she addressed them.

"Hi, everyone. I'm Ms. Thompson, but please call me Tommie. This is an advanced course and we'll be doing a fair amount of hands-on learning with a few tests and several group presentations. Most of what you learn will help you pass the National Council for Interior Design Qualification, also known as the NCIDQ exam. Passing the test is an industry standard and will certify you as a professional. The test is given twice yearly. The next one is in April of this year. I suggest you sign up now."

She went on, explaining that the classes would cover most of what was needed in order to pass the exam. This would be a short day, and she asked people in the class to introduce themselves.

"A few more items to cover before the introductions. Six of you have signed up for an internship this quarter. After class, I'll assign each of you to one of the local accredited interior design companies who have generously agreed to host you. Which one of you is Rose Shafer?" Rose raised her hand. "Because you signed up late, I'm not sure where you'll go, but don't worry, I'll find you something as soon as I can. We used to let our students choose their own internships, but not anymore. This way we know you'll be working at a reputable company.

"It's a great experience. In order to earn full credit, show up on time, work hard, and write the required paper, turning it in before the internship ends. Questions so far?"

Rose had one—where would she end up?—but Tommie would let her know.

No one else raised their hand, and she went on. "Now, we'll go around the room and introduce ourselves in five minutes per person, max. I'll call your name from the roster so I can take attendance and match your name to your face. You don't have to take the full five minutes or say much except your name and a little about yourself. I'll start.

"I opened my own interior design company when I was thirty and retired two years ago at fifty-five. My daughter, Leigh, who started working for me in college and stuck with it, handles everything now. Why did I retire so young? Two reasons. One, my marriage went south—I'm happily divorced now—and two, I lost my passion for interior design. Not the field itself, but running the business. My main interest now is to share what I know with aspiring students like yourself. Oh, and please don't ask me what my first name is. I don't like it and never use it."

Everyone laughed, including Rose, and the nervous tension often accompanying a first day of class faded.

Tommie called out the first name on the roster, which was alphabetical by last name.

While others spoke, Rose had time to think of what to say. The year and a half she'd attended the school three years earlier sounded similar to what people going ahead of her said.

She was one of the last to introduce herself. She opened her mouth to talk about her education so far, but something more personal came out. "My husband is filing for divorce," she said and promptly burst into tears.

To her surprise, everyone murmured sympathetic words. Someone handed her a tissue. She sniffled and blew her nose. "This is so embarrassing. I didn't mean to bring that up or cry. I wanted to talk about my first year and a half here three years ago and how excited I am to be back in school."

"Which you just did," Tommie said. "Divorces and breakups are never fun. I think we can all agree on that. Let's hear from the last person on the roster. Then I'll meet individually with those of you who signed up for the internship part of the curricula and hand out your internship assignments."

* * *

AFTER A PRODUCTIVE DAY, Kenny sent his crew home, as he had a tight budget and didn't want to pay overtime if possible. He stayed behind to work on a few minor things before heading out. Also, he wanted to run a few things by Rose. Wanted to check on her, solely because he knew the pain and heartache of a failed marriage. Had she enjoyed school? Made it through without breaking down?

Neither was his problem or concern, yet he wanted to know. The way she'd held her head high in an attempt to look fearless and proud when she'd met the crew had been impressive and masked her pain but didn't fool him.

A glance at his watch told him it was almost five. She'd been gone a long time and might be gone longer. He was on the verge of leaving without seeing her when he heard the garage door open. She entered through the utility room off the garage. As soon as she spotted him, she frowned. "You put in a really long day."

She didn't seem happy about that. Noted, but necessary. "It happens. Don't worry, I don't charge overtime."

"Since I'm not paying the bill, I wouldn't mind if you did." She almost smiled, putting him at ease.

"Don't worry, I'm leaving soon." His stomach growled and he laid his hand over his empty belly. "Gotta feed the beast."

"We're in the same boat," she said. "I'm super hungry myself."

"Without the noisy announcement."

"If you'd heard me in the car, you'd know differently."

"I'm planning to pick up a rotisserie chicken at Collingwood's." A grocery not far from the house.

"Those things are great."

She looked envious, and he couldn't let the comment go. "If you want, I can pick up one for you and drop it off. It's not really out of my way." It was—he lived the opposite direction—but he didn't mind.

"No, thanks. I'm going to eat leftovers and search online to check out companies where I might be interning. That's up in the air. Right now, I really need a snack. Do you like peanuts?"

He nodded. She headed into the kitchen and came back with a can of them.

"How did classes go today?" he asked when he'd swallowed a mouthful.

"I was about to ask you the same question about work," she said, then ate some herself.

"You first."

"Okay, if you really want to know. Being back in school felt good. My two classes have the same instructor, Tommie, and meet Monday and Wednesday mornings. Lots of reading and homework. The internship is Tuesdays and Thursdays, six hours per day, longer if they need me. It should be a great experience once I know where I'm going. I registered late, but Tommie's working on that. I hope to find out Wednesday."

She sounded excited, a good sign that school was the right place for her to be. "Sounds great. Interior design, right?"

"You listened the other day. I'm finishing my degree. I got busy with Peter and married life, and kinda let it go. Last week, I decided to re-enroll and did. That was before I knew about the divorce." She raised her chin again, like she wanted to fend off any negativity about that.

"Good for you, deciding to finish your degree. Also good you like being back," he said with what he hoped was an encouraging smile.

"Yes, but…" She paused and chewed her pinkie fingernail. " I really embarrassed myself. Again."

Again? "What happened?"

"Do you really want to know?"

"I wouldn't have asked if I didn't." He prompted her with a nod.

She sighed. "We went around the room introducing

ourselves and sharing about our backgrounds. I had what I wanted to say all planned out. Instead, I cried like I did yesterday around you."

He sensed her shame and felt for her. "I'm sure people understood."

"Everyone was nice, but I wish I'd held it together." She glanced down and toyed with her ponytail.

"You're not gonna beat yourself up over that, are you?"

"It's what I tend to do, especially when I come off like a weak fool."

"I'm sure that's not how people saw you."

"Tell that to my brain."

He couldn't think what to say other than a few positive suggestions. "Focus on the good stuff that happened. Tell me one thing about school today that you liked."

She seemed to think about that. "Well, there are only eleven of us in the class, which is nice, and I like my teacher. Also, I'm psyched about the internship I'll be doing—wherever it is. That starts Thursday."

"When you talk about what you enjoyed, you brighten right up. You seem better now. See? You can get past a few little tears."

"They didn't feel little to me, but I guess I can. Thanks for the tip."

"I learned it from a former boss and wanted to pass it on. I've been where you are."

"You didn't cry in front of people, though, am I right?"

"No, thank God."

"I'm going to apply for a work-study job when I'm not in class."

"I put myself through community college and my bachelor's degree that way. What job are you applying for?"

"Hold on, there," she said, looking surprised. "I had no idea you'd been in community college or that you have another degree. Where else did you go?"

"The University of Washington for a degree in construction."

"Vi and Blake both have degrees from there. That's impressive. What kind of work-study?"

"Cafeteria at both schools." Serving up food and cleaning up trays and dirty dishes had gotten old, but he was used to jobs he didn't like. He was lucky to be happy with what he was doing now, an important part of running a successful business. "I also had a partial scholarship. What are you applying for?"

"Bookstore. After class, I filled out an application and left it with someone who promised to pass it to the manager. Cross your fingers for me. Now, tell me about what you did today."

"We tore apart the powder room and started on the bathroom off the guest bedroom upstairs. We ran into a problem there."

"Oh?"

"There's a slow leak in the roof, and by the look of the damage, it's been leaking for some time. Nothing that showed up until we removed the paneling on the west wall. The drywall there is rotten and needs replacing, plus, there's mold that has to be removed. But first, the roof needs to be repaired. Let's go upstairs and I'll show you."

The bathroom was a mess. "That's not pretty. Too bad Peter and I didn't catch it."

"Like I said, we didn't see anything till we pulled off the wall. It was a slow drip, but eventually would've caused real problems."

"They seem real enough to me."

He nodded. "I turned off the water in there and let Dr. Shafer know."

"It's fine to call him Peter. I'll bet he's not happy about that."

"No one ever is. This could prolong the renovations."

"As I said before, I don't mind." She glanced up as if in thought. "Which reminds me, I'd better send him a text."

"What for?"

"He asked for daily updates on the house. It's part of the deal we made."

"Deal?"

"He's paying me to keep an eye on things. In return, I'll text him about progress, et cetera."

"I already spoke with him, so you can probably skip today."

"Knowing Peter, he wouldn't like that. He still expects to hear from me."

Kenny was learning quite a bit about the man. "I get the feeling he wasn't easy to live with."

"It wasn't that bad. He was always gone, and when he was here we tolerated each other."

Didn't sound like much of a marriage. "The roofers will be here tomorrow morning to assess the problem. Once they take care of that and we replace the drywall, we'll get back to work on that bathroom. We made decent progress on the powder room. Let's head back downstairs and you can take a look."

He showed her the room stripped of the sink, countertop,

the vinyl floor, and toilet. "You did a lot here," she said. "Please give me a heads-up before you start on the kitchen. What should I do to get it ready for you?"

"The plan is to start soon, but with the bathroom issue, I'm not sure exactly when. Can't hurt if you want to get started. Empty the cabinets and move whatever you can away from the kitchen. The dining room might be easiest to put things. We may or may not start it sometime next week."

"Good to know. Hmm… I wonder if I can hire someone to empty the kitchen. I'll ask Peter to foot the bill. If he refuses, it won't get done."

"You drive a hard bargain."

"I'll take that as a compliment. To my shock, I seem to be a natural at it. I haven't hired movers since before I moved in with Peter. Any suggestions?"

"Nothing comes to mind, but check online, read the reviews, and go from there."

"I will. Are you coming back early again tomorrow?"

"Not as early. More like eight."

"Better than seven." She sure was pretty when she smiled. She was pretty when she cried, too. "I'll be out of the house for several hours tomorrow."

He pulled his coat from the closet and shrugged into it. "Have a good evening," he said as he pulled the shoe booties off.

"You, too."

CHAPTER 5

Rose hadn't hired movers since she'd first moved out of the chaotic house where she'd grown up. She'd once been an independent woman but had grown stupidly lazy with Peter, letting him handle things like repairs and moving. A first in her life, and yes, she'd enjoyed every second without a moment's financial worry. It'd been a relief to let him take the reins. Now, it felt good being on her own again. She silently vowed to stay that way. Depend on a man? Never again.

Taking Kenny's suggestions, she googled various companies specializing in local moves and checked the ratings. Then she called YLM, short for Your Local Mover, a company with lots of five star reviews. May as well get it lined up before things got too hectic at school. She got an estimate for moving things out of the kitchen and putting them back and promised to phone the company again shortly. Within minutes of texting Peter the renovation updates and requesting money for a local mover to clear out the kitchen, she heard from him. By phone.

The last person she wanted to talk to. She let out a sigh of dread. "Yes?" she answered without a speck of warmth.

"You don't need to hire someone to move things to and from the kitchen," he told her, none too friendly, either.

"I'm not going to move that stuff, and don't you dare ask Kenny and his team to do it. They're already working hard enough. It's not their job and not mine."

"I paid you to take care of the house, and I won't give you another penny," he argued, and she pictured the no-nonsense, don't-push-me expression that'd cowed her until the day he'd dropped the divorce news in her face.

That money covered the time she'd waste handling the chores he'd left her to do, the jerk. But where shifting things around the house was concerned, she had the upper hand. "If you're going to be like that, I'll tell Kenny to skip the kitchen renovations." She was proud of her calm tone.

He tried to argue, but like before, she held firm. Without her help he'd be stuck, and he knew it. It didn't take long before he exhaled a loud, impatient breath. "Send me the invoice for it and I'll take care of it," he snapped.

One of them had lost his temper and it wasn't her. *Score a point for me.* She wanted the money now, in case he failed to come through. "That won't do. These guys, who by the way come highly recommended, expect immediate payment in cash. If you use a credit card, the price goes up to cover the credit card fee. They'll be here in the morning, and the funds have to be deposited into my account tonight."

"How do I know what to pay, when you don't know what they'll charge?"

What did he take her for, an idiot? In a way, that made sense, as throughout their short-lived marriage, when it came to problems with anything related to the house or her car, she'd played the part of damsel in distress. Well, no more.

"Give me some credit, Peter. Before I texted you, I got an estimate. They'll also want to be paid for putting what they took out back once the kitchen is done. I don't see green stickers on anything in there except your collection of beer steins. There's a lot to be moved back and forth. You need to pay up tonight. Venmo is fine."

"You're supposed to get rid of all the other stuff. It's included in what I already paid you."

Ignoring him, she mentally doubled the local company's fee to cover both kitchen moves. Then, erring on the side of caution, she tacked on several hundred dollars extra to compensate her for finding the company, making the call, and tipping the movers. She gave him the amount.

He made an unhappy sound, but at least he didn't argue anymore. "You'll have it within the hour." True to his word, he made good on that. As soon as the funds arrived in her account, she set up the move for early afternoon the following day, when she was sure to be back from her appointment with the lawyer Malcom had suggested and she'd hired.

Elated, she let out a loud "whoopie!" If she'd known Peter caved this easily, she'd have stood up to him from day one of their marriage instead of meekly agreeing to whatever he wanted whether she did or not.

She let the movers know, scheduling an early afternoon appointment, then cheered again. All in all, the day hadn't been half-bad.

Now to relax. Suddenly in the mood to get back into a designer's frame of mind—she was rusty and needed to dust off her skills before the internship started, wherever it would be—she pulled out the iPad. Playing around, she imagined the house empty and that she'd been hired to make it feel warm, inviting, and contemporary. Ideas flooded her mind, as if they'd been waiting for her to let them out. She started designing.

The next thing she knew, the device beeped, letting her know the battery was low. She'd been so involved with creating and designing diagrams that she'd worked well into the night and had fallen asleep on the sofa. She checked the time—almost six a.m.—and sprang up.

Not that she needed to. Kenny wouldn't be here for another two hours. The appointment with the attorney was two hours after that. This being a Tuesday, there was no class, but she wanted to stop by and check back on the work-study application in person, to make an impression. She could take her time showering, dressing, and eating breakfast.

With all of four hours' sleep, she should've been tired. But the elation from designing the interiors of the dining and living rooms was still with her. She could hardly wait for the first day of her internship, wherever it happened to be.

When Kenny arrived, this time minus his team, Rose frowned. "What happened to Griff, Augie, and Nell?"

"We're not able to work on the guest bathroom till the roofers take a look and we find out if patching will be enough. If it turns out I need my crew later, I'll let them know and they'll come right over." Currently, they were finishing another project he'd started before he'd lined up this one. That way, they wouldn't sit idle.

"And here, I made another big pot of coffee. Help yourself. FYI, I'll be leaving soon to stop by the community college. Then I'm meeting with my attorney. Sometime after I get back this afternoon, a local moving company will be here to move everything out of the kitchen. That way, it'll be ready when you are."

"Good to know." Kenny was impressed that she'd thought ahead. He wanted to head upstairs before the roofers showed up but decided to talk with Rose first. "You seem much better than you did when I left yesterday."

"I feel pretty good. The internship has me all excited. I can't wait to find out where I'll be going. Tommie will tell me tomorrow."

"That's great." He was familiar with the mood swings associated with the dissolution of a relationship and hoped she'd hold steady on a high. "We could work on the kitchen today, but not until you clear the stuff out. Even with local movers coming in to help, emptying the cabinets and drawers will take time."

"It'll be ready tomorrow for sure."

"I appreciate that. What if the movers show up before you get back from the lawyer's?"

"I should be finished with my appointment by then, but if I don't get back in time, let them know I'll be here soon. Peter didn't green-sticker anything in the kitchen except his collection of beer steins. Tell the people who show up what you want them to move to make it easiest to do your thing there. You mentioned storing things in the dining room, which is fine with me, as long as I can still use the fridge, et cetera, to make meals. It's okay to put stuff on the table and the buffet.

"Peter didn't sticker anything in the dining room except

the art on the walls. Ask them to keep the beer steins together. He stickered every one of those. They'll be going to California and belong in a box, which I don't have. Oh, and the long-distance movers are coming Friday. I don't have classes or the internship that day, so I'll be here. Reminder to self, make notes of where to find the green-stickered furniture and knickknacks Peter left all over the house. Which I dread."

"My crew and I will be here Friday. If for some reason you're out when they come, we'll cover for you."

"Thanks, but I'll be here. Unless something comes up."

"Got it. Peter's lucky you're willing to help."

"Which I refused to do till he compensated me. Handsomely."

"Smart."

"I guess I am."

She flashed a smile he hadn't seen that brightened the pale green of her eyes until they almost glowed. He couldn't look away, and the smile faded.

"You're staring at me. Is anything wrong?"

Plenty. She'd dazzled him into idiocy. He shook his head to clear it. "Nothing. Glad to see you looking happy. The roofers will be here soon and will probably still be here when the movers arrive to clear the kitchen."

"It's going to be a madhouse in here," she muttered and checked her watch. "Time for me to scoot. Cross your fingers about the work-study job, and wish me luck with the attorney."

She was right about the madhouse. Two roofers arrived with their truck and ladders, ready to take a look at the leak. They needed to check both the bathroom where the leak had done damage and the roof itself. While they did that, Kenny set about working on the powder room. The new counter was heavy, and it took him a while to muscle into place. Then he secured it. Next on the agenda, the sink and faucets. He attached the sink to the counter, set up the drain pipes, and tested them. He applied the grout along the sink to finish the sink, and also thought about Rose.

That smile. She'd bewitched him and didn't even know it. She was beautiful, even more so than before. She had grit, too, and strength.

Traits he admired and turned him on—a no-no. She was way too classy to look at him, plus, she had problems he couldn't fix and didn't want to.

As long as he remembered that, he saw no harm in talking to her. Face it, he didn't have a choice. She was in the same boat.

The tiles were in his truck, washed, cut to fit, and ready. He was loading them onto a dolly and was about to haul them inside when two men showed up to move the kitchen things —an hour or two ahead of schedule. Good thing she'd briefed him. He got them started, then the roofers wanted to talk. Rose also showed up ahead of schedule shortly after he'd transported the tiles inside, grueling work that caused him to sweat despite the cold day. "Hey," he said, wiping his forehead with his sleeve.

"Hi."

Nothing close to a smile this time. A visit to the divorce lawyer was rarely pleasant. "It's been busy around here."

"I see the movers have arrived."

"Earlier than scheduled. The roofers are at the store, getting the materials they need to patch the roof."

"It doesn't need replacing?"

"No, but like I said before, there's mold on the drywall where the water leaked, and it may have spread. I contacted a company to get rid of it and let Peter know."

"I'll bet he didn't like that."

"Not one bit."

"Too darn bad. I want to know what you're working on now, but I'd better introduce myself to the movers." She hung up her coat and headed into the kitchen without a second glance.

She had a lot on her mind and no reason to look at him. He got that, but was disappointed anyway. He snorted at himself. "I'll be in the powder room," he said to her back. He set the tiles on the heavy canvas he'd laid down over a plastic tarp that protected the carpeting around the powder room. If time allowed, he'd lay out the tile and grout it into place before he left this afternoon. If not, he'd do that tomorrow morning. It needed at least twenty-four to seventy-two hours to set.

He paused for a quick lunch, wolfing down a ham and cheese sandwich and glugging a lot of water, as construction work made him thirsty.

The movers finished and left. Sometime later, the doorbell rang. The roofers had come back. They got to work, and he started laying the tile on the powder room floor. The only noise in the house was his own—the radio turned down low so as not to bother Rose, and the clatter of setting the tile. Whatever she was doing, she did it quietly.

He was standing up stretching his back, when the doorbell rang again. With no idea where she'd gone, he decided to ignore it, as whoever was out there wasn't looking for him. He saw her hurry down the stairs and heard the click of the door unlocking. She was talking to someone. A man, by the sound of the voice. Kenny couldn't hear the conversation. It didn't last long.

The door locked again. Then, nothing. He ventured closer. She was standing in the entry, staring at the 9x12 envelope clutched in her hands.

She'd gone pale and her teeth gripped her bottom lip. Must've been served, he figured, wondering if someone had sued her. "You okay?" he asked.

"I don't know." She continued to stare at the envelope, tiny frown lines between her eyebrows.

He wasn't going to ask, but curiosity got the better of him. "What's in there?"

"The divorce papers."

CHAPTER 6

Rose gripped the large brown envelope. It wasn't thick or heavy, yet the weight of it bowed her shoulders. The day Peter had walked out, he'd warned her to expect the divorce papers sometime this week, so it hadn't come as a surprise. She'd assumed she'd be ready to read through it, yet for some reason, she was paralyzed and unable to open the clasp.

"Breathe," Kenny reminded her in a gentle voice. He hovered nearby, his golden-brown eyes pools of understanding.

More than grateful for the support, she pulled in a breath, then exhaled. Better. "I don't know why I'm so afraid to open this."

"It makes everything final. Unless you go to court."

"I'm aware that I can't change Peter's mind. I don't even want to. Still, this is a big change for me. He's been a part of my life for almost three years." She swallowed. "This morning, the attorney repeated what I already knew—the prenup is airtight, and we weren't together long enough for him to owe me any support. In other words, there's no point in wasting time and money trying." She toyed with the clasp holding the envelope closed, then looked to Kenny. "I've been pretty much alone for months and really haven't missed him, so why am I scared now?"

"Because any shred of hope you were holding on to is gone."

He'd hit the mark on that. She nodded, swallowed again.

"Hey, you got him to pony up money he didn't want to give you. That's pretty cool."

"Yes, but compared to what a professional would charge, he got a real bargain." She sighed and glanced at the jeans and sneakers she'd exchanged for the suit and kitten heel Manolo Blahniks after she'd come home. "I guess I should be thankful to have a roof over my head and a rent-free place to stay for a while longer."

"You're not crying, either." The corners of his lips lifted a fraction in a semblance of a smile. "Way to think positive."

She guessed so. Kenny was kind and helpful and so attractive, and she didn't want to be alone. "Will you sit with me while I open this?"

"Sure."

On the way to the living room, she paused outside the powder room to peek inside. "When I left this morning, there was no counter or sink in here, nothing but big packets of tiles outside the room. You did a lot today."

"Could've done more if I hadn't had so many interruptions," he said. "I wanted to start laying the tiles today, but that's a time-consuming job and takes a while. It'll have to wait until tomorrow. Don't touch the grout on the sink or turn on the water. You'd best stay out of the room altogether."

"I will. I'm impressed with how hard you work." She continued toward the living room. They sat down on the sofa, a roomy piece of furniture with firm cushions.

After opening the envelope, she pulled out the multiple pages of the document and read through them. "This seems pretty straightforward. My attorney said to contact him with any questions, but I don't have any. Take a look."

She passed it to Kenny. "I'm no lawyer," he said. "You should probably talk to yours."

Which would cost her more, but he had a point. "I guess I could send it to him. He has a secured link for things like this, but I doubt he'll have anything new to say. Maybe I'll run it by Malcom first—he's married to my gran and is a savvy businessman."

"Good idea." He studied her. "You're not as white as a blank sheet of paper anymore."

She hadn't realized she'd paled. "Thanks to you. You're my dose of courage."

His face reddened, as if the compliment embarrassed him. She found that endearing and adorable. "I'm here to listen and support you," he said in a gruff voice. "The courage is yours alone."

How sweet was that? "I've never thought of myself as courageous. Thank you." Overcome by his kindness, she leaned toward him, put her hands on his powerful shoulders and kissed his cheek. Nothing suggestive, just a show of appreciation. At least, she meant it to be. But he angled his head toward her, and she grazed the corner of his mouth instead of his cheek. Her instant, unwanted desire shocked her. And was wrong.

After going utterly still for a moment, he wrapped his

arms around her. So comforting and warm. How long had it been since she'd been hugged, let alone semi-kissed a man's lips? On the heels of the thought, he stiffened, let go of her and jumped to his feet as if she'd burned him. They both knew she'd crossed a boundary.

"I'm sorry," she said, inwardly wincing. "I swear, I was aiming for your cheek. I shouldn't have done that, either, and I certainly don't want anything from you. My intention was to thank you for your kindness, even if a harmless kiss that went slightly awry wasn't the right way to express that. Please don't take offense." By his stiff posture and blank expression, it seemed he definitely had. "You're a good man, and I haven't known many."

"If you had any idea what I'm thinking, you'd change your mind." He shoved his hands into his jeans pockets.

He no doubt thought she'd been coming on to him. As good-looking and buff as he was, she was too raw from the hell Peter was putting her through to think about that. Under different circumstances, yes.

Never mind that the mere touch of the corner of his mouth and the sensation of his arms around her had momentarily snuffed out her anger and hurt and set her long-deprived lady parts humming. "Should we talk more about this?"

"I don't think so. Time for me to go home. Take care."

* * *

HIS THOUGHTS IN TURMOIL, Kenny drove to his place on automatic pilot. He'd been doing all right before Rose had pressed her lips to the corner of his mouth. Should've pulled away the second her small-boned hands clasped his shoulders. She smelled great, something light, fresh, and feminine. The brief touch of the tempting lips he longed to taste and soft curves grazing his chest as he automatically hugged her had almost done him in. It was all he could do not to hold her tighter.

A vulnerable woman in the throes of a divorce. He'd come so close to making a colossal mistake. Must be out of his mind. Appalled at himself, he swore out loud and shook his head.

Nothing but trouble down that road.

At home, filled with pent-up energy despite the physically taxing day and desperate to work off his unwanted feelings, he stuffed a tee, shorts, and gym shoes and socks into a duffle bag, climbed back into the truck and headed for the Simms County Y for a grueling hour of solo handball. Exhausted at last, dripping with sweat and feeling much better, he upped his resolve to keep his distance from Rose. Because she lived in the house, he couldn't avoid her entirely, but he could avoid being alone with her.

After showering, he changed back into his jeans and flannel shirt, called the Stop on In, and ordered two burgers and a jumbo container of fries. He wolfed down the meal on the drive home. Once there, he popped a beer and texted his brother, Abe. A college freshman with a job and active social life, he was always busy. *Mom's birthday is next Monday,* Kenny reminded him. *We need to make plans. Call when you can.*

Moments later, his kid brother phoned. "Hey, Kenny. Long time. Not." Abe laughed. "I haven't talked to you since the day after Christmas."

He'd left Port Simms early that morning to go skiing with

his girlfriend, Sedona. Kenny and his mom had speculated over whether or not their relationship was serious and decided it must be. Kenny worried that he was too young for that.

"I enjoyed seeing you, Mr. College Freshman. Winter quarter started this week. Are you happy with your classes? Still planning to major in biochemistry?" Abe had been a science nerd since middle school.

"More than ever." He filled Kenny in on school. "I can't get away on Mom's actual birthday. What if I drive home the Friday afternoon before? I'm thinking we could celebrate Saturday, then I'll head back Sunday morning."

"She'd love that."

"Do you think she'll mind if Sedona comes?"

He'd never asked before. "Bringing her home to meet Mom, huh?" His turn to laugh. "I doubt she'll have any problem with that, but a phone call to her couldn't hurt. I want to meet this girl you like so much."

"She's something special."

"How serious are you?"

"Too soon to tell. Don't worry, I won't pull a Kenny and marry her yet."

Abe knew all the sordid details of his failed marriage.

"I'm glad you're taking your time." Kenny felt a pang of envy. He wanted the same thing Abe already seemed to have. Someday... They discussed the party details, which led to gift ideas.

"I don't know what to get her," his brother said. She needed money—always did—which Abe didn't have.

"Offer to do yard work or another chore next time you're home," Kenny suggested.

"That's a great idea. What are you giving her?"

"Money."

"She'll like that. If you can afford to do it, business must be good."

"Better all the time. I'm doing renovations on a house for a doctor. He hired me to get it in shape so he could net a nice profit when it sells. I went through the house with him and we discussed what he wanted. It'll cost him, but he's okay with that."

"He must be loaded."

"Yep. He's already moved to California. He promised a bonus if I get done on time."

"That could be a challenge. You and I both know problems are bound to come up. Then what?"

"I talked to him about that and made it clear that any issues could delay my finishing on time and add to the cost. He signed the contract and prepaid me thirty percent. So far, I've had to call him once about a leak in the roof and mold on the drywall. He advanced the funds that same day to cover the repair costs."

"He sounds like a good guy."

"That's what I thought. Here's where it gets weird. He never mentioned he was leaving a wife behind. Rose is her name, and she's staying in the house for now. Basically, he asked her for a divorce only a few hours before he flew to California."

"That sucks."

"It came as a total shock to me. I went in and there she was. You can imagine how stunned she was to see this strange man unlock the door and walk in. The only thing the doctor had told her was that he was leaving. He didn't give her any time to come to grips with it." Kenny still couldn't get over that. "Then I showed up."

"Sounds like you walked into a soap opera."

"It's been different." Kenny didn't expand.

"If she starts to depend on you, back away," Abe warned.

Like their mom and Buddha, Abe had watched Kenny suffer through his marriage and divorce. "Don't worry, I will. I see her almost every day, which can be difficult. She's cried a few times, but she's not sitting around feeling sorry for herself. She's in school at the community college, but otherwise she's all by herself in the house, dealing with the dust and the mess. The divorce papers arrived this afternoon, and she needed somebody to talk to."

"And you were there." Abe snorted. He didn't let the eleven-years' age difference between them get in the way of freely offering advice Kenny didn't want or need.

"Don't judge me, man," Kenny told him. "Like I said, I see a lot of her. I have no intention of getting involved with her."

"Sounds good, but why are you talking to her about her problems?"

"I don't know. It's, uh…" The way she'd raised her chin all proud and determined when it was obvious she was hurting had gotten to him. Resisting her wasn't easy. "I don't think she made a conscious decision to tell me anything in particular. At the time, I happened to be the only person around, and I guess she needed to vent. That's why." Kenny paused. "The thing is, I like her."

"That's how you started with Crystal. Mom and my dad were going through their divorce. That was awful, remember? I acted out by getting in trouble for mouthing off in school, and you reached out to Crystal. Why, I'll never know. She dumped her problems on you and expected you to bail her out—like you could help her. What a crap show. The whole thing really messed you up. Marrying her was your dumbest move ever. Divorcing her was the smartest."

"Listen to you. My little brother, spouting off like a therapist."

"Not so little. I'm a whole inch taller than you."

"Half an inch," Kenny corrected, as he always did. According to Brandy, both this father and Abe's had been tall, but having only met his birth father in his early baby years, and because Brandy had no photos of the man, Kenny had no idea what he looked like. He'd considered looking for him, but according to her he was a two-timing jerk with a nasty temper who'd never given his son a second thought. Kenny chose not to meet him.

"You're right about Crystal, though. From what I've seen of Rose, she's not like that." She had plans for herself that made her smile. "So far, anyway. Trust me, I won't let her play me. Once was enough." Only a fool would get sucked into that impossible position a second time. "See you this weekend."

"I'll call Mom now and let her know I'm coming."

CHAPTER 7

Wednesday, Rose woke up thinking about Kenny and worrying. That tiny kiss had freaked him out. She'd apologized and explained that she was simply grateful for his company. Clearly, it hadn't been enough. He must think she was out of her mind, and that didn't set well with her. She didn't want him getting the wrong idea and meant to clarify that before she left for school.

After breakfast, having no idea whether he'd bring a crew with him or not, she brewed another large pot of coffee in the mostly emptied-out kitchen. Better making a pot than not having any.

He texted as usual that he was on his way. On-edge about rehashing her apology, she considered leaving and forget talking about it, but clearing the air was important to her. She'd held her feelings in check during her entire marriage and wasn't about to do that again, not with anyone. Creating designs on the iPad calmed her, and while she waited for him she made a few touch-ups on the structural sketches. Today she planned to bring the iPad to class with her in case she needed it. She also wanted to share what she'd done with Tommie and get her feedback.

Kenny showed up with the same crew as the other day. The roofers were on their way to patch the leak. The plumbers would arrive soon, too. With the hustle-bustle of all those people around, she wouldn't be able to talk to him, not as candidly as she'd have liked. "I'll be leaving shortly," she said, clutching her iPad to her chest. As if it could give her confidence. "Do you have a minute to talk, Kenny? In the living room?"

"Okay." He didn't quite meet her gaze. Then to his crew, "Go ahead and get to work. I'll be along shortly."

He followed her into the room. "What did you want to talk about?"

Nervous, she started with something else. "Before we get to that, I wanted you to know that Malcom advised me to send the divorce papers to the attorney. I did, and he looked them over last night. Everything's in order, which means I'm going to get an uncontested divorce."

"Are you happy with that?"

"It's the only choice I have. This way, the divorce won't cost an arm and a leg and won't drag on. It'll be a relief to get it over and done with. I texted Peter and let him know."

He nodded. "What else did you want to talk about?"

Being straightforward was hard, but she needed to get it out. "I want to apologize again for last night. I shouldn't have kissed you, harmless as it was. I upset you, when I didn't mean to."

"I wouldn't call it upset. It was more than that. The thing is..." He broke off and cleared his throat. "You may not love

Peter, but you're still hurt and vulnerable. I don't want to take advantage of that."

The comment rankled, and she raised her head. "I am *not* vulnerable. Growing up, I was, but I'm not that little girl anymore. I'm more than capable of taking care of myself, and I don't need you or anyone else to watch out for me." A lesson she'd learned long ago, while Vi raised her when they were both too young to watch after themselves.

Once again, she chastised herself for falling into the habit of letting Peter take care of her. Yes, it'd been a relief, but later she'd grown colossally bored. Being a housewife was dull. True, she'd worked in retail from time to time, but that had also bored her, and she'd been a rotten employee. Although she'd stuck with Panache, even if it was only one afternoon a week, for several months now. Mainly for the cute clothes.

"I don't know what happened to you when you were a kid, but it's obvious you're able to handle the challenges in your life," Kenny said. "Doesn't mean you're bulletproof. Your soon-to-be ex-spouse left with no notice and no time for you to adjust. Even with both my ex and me wanting the divorce and setting things in motion in advance, it was still hard. I was also vulnerable. It's taken me almost two years to get past it."

She hadn't considered his view. "I'm sorry it was so difficult for you. The stuff with Peter is painful to me, too, a real blow, even if I had a hunch it was coming. In a weird way, it's also freeing. I don't have to worry about him anymore, and I feel pretty good. At least right now. I also know I'm nowhere ready to even think about another relationship."

Although after going without sex for close to a year, her hormones were alive and kicking. Kenny's arms around her had only ramped up her feelings. The heat from his body, that hard chest…Appalled at herself, she pushed the unwanted desire away. "The thing is, I feel like you and I have bonded. I guess because I dumped so much of what happened on you."

He seemed taken aback. "I wouldn't call it bonding. It's a matter of feeling comfortable together."

"You're right," she said, regretting her use of the word. "Bonding" seemed too close and intimate for two people who didn't know each other very well.

"Knowing that about yourself is a smart way to stay out of trouble," he went on.

"I guess so." She had to ask. "Now that you're healed from the past, have you met anyone special?"

"Not yet, but I'm working on it."

Then he was single. "For me, the very idea of getting into a new relationship gives me the jitters. That kiss was an innocent gesture of thanks. Thinking back, I shouldn't have done it." All of which she'd said last night, but it needed repeating.

"I won't argue with that."

He was blaming her for something that was partly his fault. "I didn't ask you to put your arms around me."

"That happened automatically and was my mistake. If you remember, I didn't hold you for long. As soon as I realized what I was doing, I let go."

She needed more information. "I don't understand why you hugged me in the first place."

He glanced upward, as if composing what to say. "Because I wanted to."

Since he was being honest… "I enjoyed it, too, for the second or so it lasted, but it's way too soon for me to be hugging any man." She gnawed on her pinkie nail, but it was mostly chewed off, so she switched to her thumb. Then caught herself and stopped. "Or touching you at all, regardless of the reason."

He blew out a breath. "It's good the whole thing is out in the open."

"Absolutely. Let's forget it happened. That way, we won't feel tense around each other."

"Forget *what* happened?" he said with a slightly crooked smile that charmed her.

He glanced at the iPad. "You've been holding onto that like you're drowning and it's your life raft. Whatcha got in there? Unless it's none of my business."

"Nothing private. For practice, I've been playing around with designing the interiors of some rooms in this house." On impulse, she added, "This is purely structural, so you'll have to use your imagination. I haven't shown it to anyone yet, but I wouldn't mind your opinion—if you're interested in taking a look."

"I'd like to, but I don't have time right now. And you should get to class. How about a rain check for this afternoon, before I leave for the day? By then, the plumber should be finishing up, and the mold removal team taking care of doing what they need to get rid of it. Hopefully the roofers will also be making progress, and my crew, too."

She checked her watch. "Whoa, it's later than I thought. I'm not sure when I'll be home, but I'll be here for sure midafternoon. I'll show you then. I'm crossing my fingers all goes well with the plumber and roofer."

"It should. Have a great time at school. I hope you get placed with a great design company."

"Me, too."

She drove to class with a smile in her heart. Kenny had accepted her apology and she'd accepted his. All was well.

* * *

As soon as Kenny checked on his crew upstairs, Augie eyed him. "Does Rose have a thing for you?"

"No," Kenny assured him.

"Do you for her?"

"Absolutely not." A bald-faced lie. He was strongly drawn to her but wasn't about to do anything about it. Ever. "Where's this coming from?"

"Just saying what we all saw," Augie answered. "Tell him, Nell."

The sole female on the crew and unlike Augie not yet on the payroll—though Kenny planned to make all three of his hourly crew permanent hires as soon as the budget allowed—hesitated. "Don't worry," Augie assured her. "Kenny isn't gonna get mad. He never does unless we call in sick too many times or decide to skip work at the last minute."

She remained silent and wary until Kenny sighed. "You may as well tell me."

"Since you asked, okay. The way you look at each other, and the, I don't know, the feelings we all sense. At least I do."

Augie and Griff nodded in agreement.

"She's going through bad times." Curious looks all around, and he realized he'd forgotten to tell them. "I should've explained and didn't. Last Friday, her husband walked out on her. He's filed for divorce and plans to sell the house right out from under her. It's a nasty situation to be in. That's why I'm careful to be extra nice around her." Which was the absolute truth, just not all of it.

"Oh, man," Nell said. "That's horrible."

Griff scratched his head. "What's she going to do?"

"She'll have to move out before the house goes on the market."

"I hope she sues his butt," Nell said. "I would."

Not wanting to get into the gory details, Kenny shrugged. "Not our business. Time to get back to work. The plumber should be here soon, so clear out any debris before he turns the water off. Once the mold removers set up their heater fans in there and shut the door to dry out the mess, we won't be able to work in there. You head downstairs and start on the kitchen. I'll be in the powder room downstairs laying the tile floor."

Soon after he carted a load of tile into the powder room, the plumber showed up. Kenny took him upstairs and showed him signs of the water damage and mold. "Any questions, come find me on the main floor."

Between talking with the plumber once that job was done and checking that the mold removal people were hard at work, texting Peter with the amount due, answering questions from the plumbers and roofers, and laying tile on the main floor, the day flew by. Shortly after four, he sent his team home. The kitchen was a mess, a sure sign of progress. His back hurt from laying out the tiles, but a good portion of that work was done. Tomorrow, he'd finish up with that and grouting the tiles in place, painstaking work that'd take several hours.

As he put tools away and cleaned up as best he could, the front door opened. Rose was home. He was way too glad to see her, and that bothered him. Maybe he'd skip looking at the stuff on her iPad she'd wanted to show him.

He headed toward the entry with his tools to tell her he was leaving. She'd paused there and gave an unhappy frown. "This place is a mess. Would you mind holding my purse and iPad while I hang up my coat? I really don't want to put them on the floor."

Not even a courteous hello? She wasn't happy to see the house or him. That stung, but better this way. "Hand me your stuff," he grumbled.

She squinted at him. "Bad day?"

"No, a pretty good one."

"Then why are you scowling?"

He shrugged. "You frowned, I scowled back."

"Excuse me for not smiling when I opened the door and saw the dirty mess everywhere."

"This is what happens during renovations. Some people stay away from the property during that time, but you can't. I cleaned up as best I could. By the way, don't go into the powder room. I laid the tiles, but I haven't secured them."

"Got it. I need an update for the day for my report to Peter. By the way, the bookstore work-study job has been filled. So have all the others."

"That's a shame. I'm sure you'll find something." He told her about the plumber, the heat fan, and the newly repaired roof. "Peter already knows all this—I talked to him twice. The repair costs are more than we thought."

"I'll bet he didn't like that anymore than he did the other day."

"Not at all, but he doesn't have much choice." He nodded at her jacket, still under his arm. "Gonna hang this up?"

"I was about to." She took it from him and put it away. "I'll take my iPad back now. I have to tell Peter what you already told him."

"Right, he expects daily updates. Or, you could let him know that since I contacted him, there's nothing more to report. By the way, the kitchen is all torn up. We put the fridge and microwave in the dining room. The oven is in the utility room. You won't be able to use it. You can tell him about that."

"Oh. As long as I have the fridge and microwave, I'll be all right."

He picked up his tool case. Disappointment radiated from her. "You're leaving. I thought—never mind."

Now she seemed hurt. So many different emotions in the past few minutes, a good reminder that she was dealing with a tough situation and he didn't want to get involved with her. Yet, he couldn't go, not this way. He set the case down. "Going home can wait. Show me those drawings."

CHAPTER 8

On the way to the living room, the only relatively uncluttered place to sit besides the den or the upstairs bedrooms, Rose stopped to peek into the powder room. "I really like that floor."

"Once the grout dries and I clean it up, it'll be pretty. When I repaint the walls and ceilings, it'll be even better."

"As soon as it's finished, I'll take a photo for Peter."

"You sure are nice to him."

"When he's a jerk? I know."

She felt bad about greeting Kenny with a frown when he had nothing to do with her irritation. "I didn't mean to walk through the door in a sour mood. I had no reason to. The mess caught me off-guard when I should know better. I've lived here since Peter proposed, and I'm used to coming home to a house exactly as I left it—neat and tidy. I wasn't always so fussy, but I learned to be. If things weren't in their 'right' place, he'd get surly. He's a surgeon and used to things just so."

"He wasn't easy to live with, huh? I'm lucky I never had that problem. I grew up with a single mom and we got along pretty well. I shouldn't have reacted the way I did, either. This was a long day and it's been a while since lunch."

She was hungry, too, but after the kiss misunderstanding, sharing a meal seemed too familiar.

"I didn't think about that. I won't keep you long, I promise. I'll smile a lot, too, because this was a stellar day."

"By all means, tell me about it."

He seemed more interested than Peter ever had, and she shared it all. "After class, I stayed behind and showed Tommie what I'd created on the iPad. We looked at everything and talked about it.

"She was super impressed, so much so that she offered me a internship at her business, Thompson Bespoke Interior Design, instead of the one she'd arranged for me to go to. Her daughter, Leigh, runs it now. We drove over there. It's such a cool place—a decent size with plenty of design books and samples. Lots of color and style options for tiles and flooring, paint colors and types, wallpaper, furniture supply books, window dressing, and more.

"Leigh liked my drawings, too, and apparently me. Said she'd be happy to have me in the shop. She's smart, and I think I'll learn a ton from her." Rose couldn't stifle a note of excitement.

Kenny chuckled, a pleasant sound, then flashed a grin that crinkled the corners of his eyes. "It's good to see you happy. Show me the drawings that blew those two women away."

He was good-looking no matter what, but when he smiled like that, well, butterflies fluttered in her stomach. Wary of sitting beside him on the living room sofa, she pointed toward the den, aka Peter's former home office. "We need a table to sit at. There's one down the hall." Everything he'd green-stickered—the file cabinet and electronics devices, paintings, and the Herman Miller Aeron chair—would be loaded onto the moving van Friday. The printer, desk, and square wood table and chairs where she wanted to sit would be left behind. Hmm… maybe she'd take them with her to wherever she ended up living. If there was enough space. Or store it somewhere if she could afford it.

They sat in chairs at ninety degrees to each other, which felt safe and not too cozy.

Self-conscious about sharing her work with Kenny despite her eagerness to show him what she could do—he might not like it—she pushed her concerns aside, opened the iPad, and slid it toward him. "This is how I envision the living room in this house if I had free reign. Keep in mind, it's only a layout, aka a strategic sketch. Depending on the client, I'd either leave it in black and white or use their color scheme. I colorized the pieces in my drawing for the heck of it."

He stared silently at the screen for so long, she began to think he hated it, but didn't know how to tell her. "If you don't like it…" she said and trailed off.

"Are you kidding? No wonder Tommie and Leigh got so excited. What you've done is amazing. Your spatial skills are something special. I like these colors, too. You transformed the existing living room into something modern, comfortable, and not fussy. You're really good at this."

She felt all happy and warm inside. "This entire house is fussy. That's all Peter. I've always wanted to change the décor and offered to move things around, use different fabrics, and paint the walls a different color, but he wouldn't hear of it. After a long time away from using the design app, I was a little rusty, but the tools and techniques came back to me pretty quickly." As if her mind had been waiting for her to realize how much the work mattered to her and had burst into her imagination. "I had a great time with it."

"That shows in your work. You should be proud of yourself."

She beamed at him. "Thanks. I am."

"I'd hug you, but that's probably a bad idea. Will you settle for a hi-five?"

That felt safe and was. But a part of her wanted that hug.

"Have you done other designs?" he asked.

Better send him on his way before she initiated the hug and got herself into trouble. He was comfortable around her again, and she wasn't about to jeopardize that. "Yes, but we're both hungry and tired. My internship starts tomorrow. I'll be up early, getting ready and will probably leave shortly after you get here.

"I'll be working Tuesdays and Thursdays, which you already know, for six hours at a time. And they're paying me!" Even saying the words felt great. She wouldn't earn much, but a little was better than nothing. "Then I'm meeting my two best friends for dinner. Eating out isn't in my budget, but I'm in the mood to celebrate and so looking forward to being with them. I won't get home till late. If you want to see more of my work, I'll show you Friday."

"Sounds good. 'night."

After he left, Rose microwaved a frozen dinner she'd taken from the freezer part of the fridge—ugh. Not her preferred way to cook or eat, but it worked for now. When she finished, she texted Peter about the kitchen. No sense boring both him and herself repeating the guest bathroom update. She added that Kenny continued to work hard and was doing a good job. As always, Peter replied with a thumbs-up emoji.

She realized how good it felt to share the internship news with a man who genuinely delighted in it and cheered her on. She'd never had anything close to that with Peter. Then, because she was bursting to also share the internship goings-on with the people closest to her and didn't want to wait till dinner the following evening, she group-texted her besties and Vi, who was due home on Sunday, yay! Last, she phoned Gran.

Gran was thrilled for her, and Vi and her girlfriends replied with exclamation points and grinning emojis.

She fell asleep with a smile on her lips and in her heart.

ROSE DIDN'T HAVE to show up at Thompson's until ten o'clock Thursday morning, but she left the house not long after Kenny and his team arrived. As much as she enjoyed seeing him, the work crew was loud and noisy and messy, making it difficult to focus on anything. With almost two hours to spare and her imagination running wild, she decided to scout around for a place to live. She wouldn't have to move out for six weeks give or take, but it couldn't hurt to check prices online and scout around.

Rents were higher than they'd been when she'd last lived in an apartment. Yikes. She definitely needed to find a part-time job, both to earn money and as proof to a landlord that she'd have the income to pay the rent. That and roommates. Hopefully, she'd find a house with an available room.

As for a job, why not call the manager at Panache?

Although Rose hadn't exactly been an exemplary employee, taking unscheduled days off and not always punctual. She doubted they'd give her more hours, but she'd give them a call.

Refusing to let a lack of steady income or the prices of housing get her down, she showed up at Thompson's thirty minutes ahead of schedule—better that than showing up late. "Am I too early?" she asked/

"Not at all." Leigh let her in with a grin, which she returned. "Welcome. Let me show you where to hang your coat and stow your things. Then we'll get right down to business."

Such a cute place. Big enough to explore and consult with customers in relative privacy.

"You'll want to familiarize yourself with our samples and the various interior design books on the bookshelf," Leigh said. "Anytime a customer needs ideas or seems at a loss, suggest they look through one or two.

"You'll find that every customer is different. Some know exactly what they want, while others have no idea and look to you for help. Answer questions, and if the customer seems serious, you'll probably want to take a look at their home. That's a good time to access what they already have and find out what they want to change. Never second guess. Ask questions that help the customer focus."

It sounded difficult. "I'll probably take notes," Rose said.

"I do that, too. Just make sure your focus is on them, not your notebook. I have an appointment this morning with a client, Mrs. Clinton—as a high-end company, we refer to our customers as clients—and you're welcome to join us today. She won't mind at all." She checked her watch. "It's almost time to open. One last comment. We're all pretty experienced here, so any questions you have, find one of us and ask."

She unlocked the door and three women and one man, all of them older than Rose, entered the store. "Come with me and I'll introduce you."

Rose committed their names to memory. Katya, black hair pulled back; Belle, blonde with bangs; Rich, tall and thin like a bean; and Arlene, in her early fifties and full of energy and smiles. They seemed friendly. They went into the employee-only room, poured coffees, and reviewed the schedule.

"Time to open," Leigh announced and switched the closed sign to open. "Mrs. Clinton should be here anytime now. There she is. Listen and learn."

Rose did exactly that. When the store was quiet, which wasn't often, she paged through the design books, looked at various samples—there were so many, getting familiar with them would take a ton of time—learned how various apps worked to colorize walls and flooring, and other things.

So much to learn. The six-hour shift ended before she knew it. She left the store both overwhelmed and elated. She wouldn't be bored here.

She could hardly wait to talk to Ragan and Pressley. Mostly, though, she wanted to share with Kenny.

CHAPTER 9

There were times when a girl had to splurge, and this was one of them. On the east side of town, seated at a table with Ragan and Pressley at McPherson's Diner, and high on life for the moment, Rose enthusiastically shared the details of her first day as an intern. "I'm so psyched! Everyone is nice, and I learned tons." She paused to sip her drink and nibble her salad. "You had paid internships and so do I, but I'm only working twelve hours total per week. Which means I'll need to find a job."

"Hey, it's a start," Pressley said. "I'm not surprised you're excited. That company has a great reputation."

Ragan nodded. "I've driven by countless times but haven't gone in."

"You should both come visit. The customer service is top-notch. Employees refer to customers as clients. Is that cool, or what?"

"It's professional," Pressley commented.

They continued talking business until the main course arrived. Then the talk turned to personal matters. "How are things with Jonathan?" Rose asked. The guy Pressley had been dating for several months.

She made a face. "So-so."

"You're getting tired of him," Rose guessed.

Her friend nodded. "I don't think we'll be together much longer. How are you doing, Rose? I know you're happy about the internship, but otherwise?"

"I've been thinking about that, too," Ragan said. "You don't seem nearly as upset about Peter as you were when we last saw you."

"Tonight I'm doing really well, but I have my ups and downs. I never realized how hard it was to live with him. Even when he was gone, I felt restricted. Except when I was out of town myself. I feel like I can breathe again."

"Money can't compensate for love and attention, am I right?"

"Yes, but money's nice to have. Anyway, Kenny saw one of my design sketches—an in-color spatial depiction of Peter's living room with more modern furniture and warmer wall color and really liked it. It's so nice to have a man interested in what I'm doing. Peter never was."

Ragan and Pressley shared a look, and Pressley leaned toward Rose. "Speaking of Kenny, how is he?"

"He seems fine, and why wouldn't he be? He has a team he trusts and makes good money. I, on the other hand..." Wanting to share and clear up the confusion she'd been dealing with since the kiss-not-a-kiss, Rose told them everything. "Kenny was there when I got the divorce papers the other day. I was a basket case. Which is weird, as I'm not at all sorry about the divorce. I'll be glad when we're officially exes."

She paused, and both women nodded. "There I was, all

upset. His team was gone, but he was still working. As I told you before, he used to be married. He understood my reaction to those papers and was great, mostly listening, but he also chimed in and really helped me feel better. When I was calm again and he was ready to leave, I—" Rose paused and lowered her voice. "I meant to kiss his cheek to thank him for being there. Instead, I accidentally kissed the corner of his mouth. He sorta hugged me." Her face went hot.

"Whoa. A kiss on the side of his mouth. Things are really heating up," Pressley teased.

"Doesn't sound that way, does it? But we both felt something. Of course, it won't go anywhere. It can't. I'm nowhere close to starting anything. Kenny wouldn't, anyway. He says I'm vulnerable and doesn't want to take advantage of that. I swore I wasn't—I'm not, I mean—but maybe I am?"

"Of course, you are," Ragan soothed. "Anyone in your shoes would be."

Pressley nodded. "Just don't fall in love on the rebound," she warned. "That never works."

"I won't. That's the last thing I want or need." True, yet she couldn't stop thinking about Kenny and wondering what would've happened if he hadn't let her go.

They chattered on. After dessert sometime later, Rose was ready to go home. The three of them embraced and said their goodnights.

* * *

FRIDAY MORNING, Kenny showed up at the house ahead of his crew. He wanted to hear about Rose's first day as an intern and check on her state of mind. She was on the sofa in the living room, eating breakfast from a bowl on her lap. "You're earlier than I expected," she said. "It's a good thing I'm dressed. But then, you've seen me in my robe."

That he had. "Forgot to text you this morning." He felt bad about that, but she waved the comment away.

"No problem. Where are the rest of the crew?"

"They'll be along shortly. What time are the movers expected?"

"Sometime this morning. It'll be good to get rid of Peter's boxes and the other stuff he's waiting for."

"How was your first day of internship?"

"Really great. Get yourself some coffee and I'll tell you about it." When he sat down moments later, careful to leave plenty of space between them, she was finishing her cereal. "Thanks for leaving me a note about your progress yesterday. I peeked in at the powder room. Don't worry, I didn't step on the floor. It looks really nice." She yawned. "Then I texted Peter."

"Out late, were you?" he teased.

"I got to talking with Ragan and Pressley, and the time got away from us. But I didn't mind. I enjoy being with them."

Her high energy and good mood made him smile.

"What are you smiling about?" she asked, doing the same thing herself.

"Seeing you happy brightens the day." That sounded corny, almost romantic. He hadn't meant it that way and quickly added, "What I mean is your enthusiasm is contagious."

"I'm glad to know that. Hard to believe I feel this good. I have more energy than I have in ages and haven't shed a single tear in two days. I'm having too much fun."

He liked the positive swing she'd taken. "Then you're pleased with the internship?"

"Super psyched. The staff are nice and full of helpful information, and I enjoy interacting with customers. I told Ragan and Pressley to stop by and take a look at Thompson's sometime. You should, too."

"I will. I don't need their services now, but as my business grows, I'll need a company like theirs to help clients with decorating. Especially if I decide to build new homes."

Her eyes widened. "You're going to do that?"

"That's been my long-term plan, but I also enjoy working on existing houses. Like this one."

"Are you saying this is your first renovation?"

The first where he'd bonded with the person who lived there. "I've done a few." Including his own, which wasn't finished yet. "Renovations don't take as much work as building from scratch. That requires permits for everything and a lot of money up front with no promise of whether I'll come out ahead."

"I never thought about those things. You sure are good at it."

"I appreciate that." He was beginning to think specializing in renovations and remodels instead of new construction might be the way to go.

"Back to Thompson's and your future customers," she said. "Referrals are always welcome."

"Look at you, already selling the company."

A caught-me smile bloomed on her face. "When you do come in, be sure to tell the boss, Leigh." She stood. "I don't have classes today, but Tommie has office hours this morning and I want to talk to her about the internship and get her recommendations on which antique stores might like the stuff Peter left here. After that, I'll visit a few with the photos I snapped, which could take a while. When the movers show up, ask them to check every room for green stickered items and boxes. Peter's paying them directly, so you don't have to do anything else. I'll be home later this afternoon. I'll show you more drawings when you finish work—if you're still interested."

He was, and not only in the drawings, way more than was smart. "I'll look forward to it."

He walked her to the door. As she put on her coat, they shared a long look. Her expression told him she wanted more than eye contact. She wasn't alone in that. But acting on it was too risky. He cleared his throat. "Good luck with the antiques."

"Fingers crossed." She grabbed her things and left.

CHAPTER 10

Rose could tell Tommie was surprised to see her. "What brings you to school on a Friday?"

"Two things. First, I want to thank you for giving me a chance to work at Thompson's. It's an amazing company. I feel lucky to be there."

Tommie beamed. "Leigh is impressed with your enthusiasm and people skills."

Pleased to hear that and not wanting to take up too much of her instructor's time, she moved on to the second reason for stopping by. She asked for names of the best antique sellers in town.

In her car, she phoned Robie Antiques, Tommie's top recommendation, to find out if they'd look at the photos she'd taken. Bill Robie, the owner, readily agreed to look at them. Hopefully, she'd be able to get rid of most of what Peter had left behind.

The antiques store was a ten-minute drive from Town Center, aka downtown Port Simms, and was located near a contemporary furniture store and another selling home furnishings. A bell over the door of Robie Antiques chimed as she entered. Instead of the junk and clutter found in other antique shops, this one was neat and organized and to her eye, the pieces high quality. At the moment, she was the sole customer. A tall male with keen eyes who looked to be in his late forties approached her. "I'm Bill," he greeted. "You must be Rose."

To her delight, after studying the photos, he asked to come over and take a look at the actual pieces. Rose explained about the disrupting construction, and he decided to stop by when the workers weren't around. They settled on Monday around five.

He handed her his card and shook her hand. She couldn't help but compare his handshake with Kenny's that first day. Both were firm and businesslike, but Kenny's had felt warm and comforting. She was starting to like him more and more, and the dangers of getting involved on the rebound preyed on her mind and dimmed her upbeat mood. Kenny was a friend she enjoyed talking with, she reminded herself. Nothing more.

She arrived home early in the afternoon, hungry for lunch and with a strong sense that her life was definitely on the upswing. Griff and Nell were busy tearing up the kitchen. She greeted them, and they let her know the movers had come and gone. This was good news.

Upstairs, she changed into jeans and a comfortable pullover sweater—now that she was interning at Thompson's, she felt the need to dress up even to stop by Tommie's office. The movers had taken the antique dresser and all the art from the master bedroom, and for the past few days she'd been emptying the dresser and storing the clothing she'd kept there in boxes along the wall. Not fun, but easier to move when the time came. The bed, not an antique, was still there. She hoped to sell it somewhere.

The guest bathroom, with new pipes and zero mold, had a new wall and a coat of primer. In the same room, Kenny and Augie were working on the walk-in shower. She peeked in to say hi. "I hope the movers weren't too much trouble."

"None at all. They had a list of what Peter wanted them to pick up and seemed pretty thorough."

"Let's hope they got everything. I'll be in what was the den," she said before returning downstairs.

After eating a PB&J sandwich, she took the iPad into the den and worked on different drawings. She couldn't wait to show them to Kenny and talk about the class, the upcoming antique dealer's visit, and his day, none of which would happen for several hours.

On a high from the visit with Bill Robie and the good things in her life, she decided to phone Melinda, her boss at Panache, the boutique where she worked four hours per week, and ask for a few more days and regular hours. She'd didn't want to work there, but she needed a job, and soon.

The last time she'd spoken to Melinda, she'd called in sick, due to Peter turning her world upside down. Had it only been a week ago? It felt like ages. She took a deep breath, then punched in the number. The phone rang and rang before the call went to voice mail. The boutique must be super busy, which hopefully meant they were swamped and needed her to come in more often. She left a message with the days she'd be available, then disconnected.

She itched to call Vi and update her on everything, but that could wait until she and Blake returned from their honeymoon on Sunday. Rose could hardly wait. Wanting to set up a dinner together, she phoned Gran. "Well, hello, you," her grandmother said. "How are you doing, honey?"

"Better than I was the last time we talked

"You sound that way. You must like school."

"A lot." Rose filled her in on the internship. Then added, "Vi and Blake come back Sunday."

"She's treating you to dinner, right?"

"A week from this coming Tuesday. I'm thinking our family should get together sometime after that."

"That'd be wonderful. Talk to Vi about it and set a date. Malcom and I will meet you anywhere."

No sooner had the call ended than Melinda phoned. "I was glad to hear from you," she said. "We've been busy and I could really use your help. But you have to promise to stick to a schedule."

"As long as we can work around my classes and internship, I will." With those in mind, Rose agreed to work eight-hour shifts on Fridays and Saturdays, and four hours Sundays beginning tomorrow, which added up to twenty hours a week.

Thanks to living frugally, she still had a respectable amount of cash in her bank account, at least until she had to make withdrawals for rent payments. Not enough to last forever, but add in the funds from the pieces she hoped to sell —positive thinking—and she ought to be able to manage the rent wherever she lived. Even if she wasn't excited about spending Fridays and weekends at Panache, knowing she had more hours took a weight off her shoulders. Besides, having worked at jobs she didn't like in the past, she knew she could do this.

She could always sell the jewelry but wasn't ready to part with it. Except for the wedding ring. She was ready to get rid of the thing. Why not keep the diamond and save it till she had money to use it in a different piece. Something to think about.

Humming, she turned on the iPad and began a sketch of what was left of the den. Too bad she couldn't transform the house, which would net more money when it sold. But it wasn't hers, and she wouldn't get a thing for fixing it up. The staging people would handle the cosmetics. She stopped thinking about this house and started working on an imaginary one.

Soon after, she set the iPad down. Friday night was just around the corner, and she had no plans for how to spend it. Forget sitting around the house and spending the evening streaming something. She wanted to be around people. What to do?

She was thinking about that when Kenny knocked on the den door and poked his head inside. "The crew are gone till Monday. Why don't I show you what we did today for your update to Peter. You can't go in yet—we haven't grouted the tiles—but you can look. Then you can tell me what happened at the antique shop and show me what you've been drawing."

Fine with her, and she stood and followed him up the steps. With him leading the way, she was free to admire the view of the big man's broad shoulders and strong, muscular arms and legs, at least what she could see of them. Cute rear end, too. *Stop that right now*, she silently cautioned and averted her eyes to her right hand and then her left.

With bi-monthly manicures, she kept her nails in great shape. They didn't look so good now. Thanks to moving furniture and a bad case of nerves that led to gnawing on her pinkies and thumbs, much of the polish was either chipped or chewed off. Rose was horrified. How could she have been so careless to let that go, when she wanted to present her best self at Thompson's and Panache? What would she do when her hair needed shaping and the subtle platinum streaks needed freshening? Those things cost money she couldn't afford to spend. For now, her hair looked decent enough.

But the nails… Thankfully, she had a decent stash of manicure tools, polish in several colors, and polish remover in the bathroom. She made a mental note to fix the problem later tonight.

She was so busy frowning at her hands, she didn't watch where she was going. At the top of the stairs, she bumped into Kenny and almost tumbled backwards down them.

"Whoa," he said, pivoting toward her and firmly clasping her upper arms. "You okay?"

Her face felt hot. "I'm so embarrassed. I wasn't watching where I was going."

"That's dangerous, especially on stairs."

More dangerous still was the warmth of his hands on her arms, his intent gaze on her, and the sudden flare of desire in her female parts. "You're right." Fighting the urge to step closer and do something she'd regret, she pulled out of his grasp. "I was distracted."

"I feel pretty distracted myself," he muttered. Turning away as if he couldn't look at her again, he strode toward the guest bathroom.

* * *

WANTING to keep his distance from Rose, Kenny silently swore as he reached the partly renovated bathroom. He'd almost lost it. She wasn't easy to resist with her soft curves dangerously close. The longing in her eyes, her fresh, sweet scent and slightly parted lips had teased his senses to the point that he'd almost given in to what he wanted. To taste and touch her...

He gave himself a mental smack in the head. She was in no shape to get involved with him. He didn't want to get tangled up with her that way, either. Tell that to his revved-up body and hammering chest. Careful to stand apart from her, he waited while she checked out the progress on the bathroom.

"That's pretty. Maybe I should take a photo of it and send it to Peter."

"Wait until the tile's grouted and dry and the room is painted," he advised in a voice harsh to his own ears.

"When do you think you'll finish?" She spoke the words to the bathroom, not him, proving she was as uncomfortable about the collision as he was. Good, that made steering clear easier.

"Sometime next week. Once we get things shipshape, we'll start on the master bath."

Her head swiveled toward him, this time with a pained expression. "Let me know when, and I'll get my stuff out of there."

He figured she was too pressed for time for any moving right now. "I get it—you're busy with work and school. If you need more time to transfer your things, we'll focus more on the kitchen."

"I don't mind switching bathrooms. It's what follows later

that I dread. Finding a place to live that fits my budget means getting rid of some of my stuff. That won't be fun."

Then, almost as if she felt guilty, she hastily added, "I sound like a snob, don't I? I'm not, I swear."

Having seen her at her worst when her husband suddenly walked out and then all lit up telling him about her first day as an intern made that obvious. He gestured toward the stairs and followed her from a safe distance. "That's what storage units are for—to house the stuff you want to keep."

"I'll do that if I can afford it." When they reached the main floor, she went on. "In case you wondered, I grew up in a small house. When I met Peter, I was living in a one-bedroom apartment with a closet my roommate and I took turns using as a second bedroom. In the housing department, I'm moving backward." She bit her thumbnail for a moment before raising her chin. "I'll adjust soon enough. Let's sit in the former den. That's where I left my iPad."

They sat at the table and took the same seats as before. "You've had more than your share of sudden changes," he said. "Trust me, I know about adjusting to change."

"After your divorce?"

"Long before I met my ex. Brandy—that's my mom's name —got pregnant with me when she was about to graduate from high school. She and my birth father got married right away. That turned out to be a big mistake. According to her, he had a nasty temper. He walked out before my second birthday. I have no memory of him at all." Not wanting to bore her, he went silent.

"Do you ever see him?"

"No, and I'm fine with that."

"Then what happened?" she asked.

"When I was eleven, my mom married Mitchell, a really great guy. That same year, she had another baby, Abe. He's a freshman at the UW now. I liked my stepdad and considered him my father. They split up when I was at the UW. I was twenty-two. That was a real shock." Devastating. They'd seemed so happy. Being away in college, he hadn't had a clue. It'd done a real number on Abe, too. For a while, Kenny had driven home on weekends to hang out with his brother, who'd been lost.

"When do your marriage and divorce fit into that?"

"You ask a lot of questions," he said, tired of the conversation. Rehashing the past was no fun.

"I tend to do that when I'm curious. Don't answer if you'd rather not."

Because she seemed to want to know, he shrugged. "I don't mind." Anyway, he had nothing to hide. "I met Crystal at an engagement party about two years after my Mom and Mitchell divorced. She seemed nice and we got along okay. She depended on me a lot." Way too much. "I was flattered, I guess. I wanted a family and kids, and I picked her. Big mistake." He eyed her. "We finished here?"

She nodded. "You really have been through changes. Tough ones. I'm sorry."

Her heartfelt look was a lot like pity. He squared his shoulders. "I survived, and I'm doing really well. Now."

"You don't have to convince me of that. You're not the only one who had a tough time growing up."

"How so?" She hesitated and he added, "I told you mine, now tell me yours."

"If you really want to know… When my sister, Vi, and I were little, our parents mostly left us to fend for ourselves.

Being five years older than I am, she basically raised me. When our parents divorced, our gran helped out as best she could. She was a big help, but we were still on our own a lot. Like you, we made it through. Ugh, I don't like talking about that any more than you did."

"I know someone with that same name—Blake's girlfriend, Vi."

"That's my sister. She mentioned that she met you once at Blake's place. By the way, she's not his girlfriend anymore. They got married."

He grinned at the news. "Isn't that something? I'm not surprised, though. They seemed pretty crazy about each other."

"Yes, but they didn't plan to marry for a while. Then she got pregnant. They tied the knot a few weeks ago."

Kenny suffered a twinge of envy. "Lucky them. Like I said, I want a family and kids, too."

"No kids for me, thanks."

He'd never heard that from any of the single women he knew. "You don't like children?"

"I mean, I'm happy for Vi and Blake, but having some of my own? Uh-uh."

He had no idea why that bothered him, but it did. "If this is too personal, tell me to butt out. Why don't you want kids?"

"My chaotic upbringing. The reason my parents neglected us was because they were busy partying and fighting with each other. The rest of the time, they worked." Rose's grimace showed what she thought of that. "Raising me wasn't easy, and my hat goes off to Vi for that. Our gran helped some, but mostly it was just the two of us. Like I said, I'm happy for my sister, but I can't see myself as a mother."

And here he'd thought being raised by a single mother for eleven years was tough. "You've also been through a lot."

She shrugged. "Like you, I survived. I guess that's something. I have so much to tell you about my day, if you're interested."

"I sure am. I also want to see more of those drawings."

She lit up, a beautiful thing to see. He wanted to bask in her light.

"You're leaning halfway across the table, like I'm about to share something huge," she said. "It's not that momentous."

Watch yourself, he silently ordered and sat back. He wasn't about to admit how drawn he was to her. "Is this better?"

She nodded. "I'll start with my day and share the drawings later. I went to talk to Tommie—she has office hours on Friday. She had good feedback for me about my first day at Thompson's. She started that company. Her daughter, who runs it now, told her I fit right in. You have no idea how good that feels!"

She was glowing, joy radiating from her. Impossible to resist. It was all he could do to sit still, when he wanted to pull her to her feet and kiss her. Good thing she couldn't read his mind. "That's great," he managed in his normal voice.

"The day gets even better. Before I forget, if you plan to come back tomorrow, that's okay with me, but if you don't, that's fine, too. I'll be at Panache all day."

"What's Panache?"

"The boutique where I've been working on and off. I'll need funds for rent and expenses, so I signed up for regular hours. My shifts are eight hours on Fridays and Saturdays, and four on Sundays."

On top of school, the internship, finding a new apartment,

and moving? She'd taken on a lot. "And that's a good thing?" he asked.

"It'll be a big help and turned out to be great timing. I called my boss a little while ago, and she seemed pleased to hear from me. I earn commission on any sales I make there, and I'm pretty good at selling."

"I'll bet." He had a hunch she could sell ants if she needed to. With her mesmerizing light and enthusiasm, he imagined everyone wanted to be touched by it.

"I expect to earn decent money. "Not enough to cover all my expenses, but between what I earn from the internship and the boutique and with careful budgeting I should be okay. Here's the next piece of good news—cross your fingers for me. I met with an antique furniture buyer and showed him photos of the stuff Peter left behind. He's stopping by late Monday, after you and your crew are finished for the day, to look at and hopefully buy at least some the antiques Peter left behind. The pieces he sells are high quality. So are the things Peter left behind. I hope he likes what he sees." She paused. "I'm talking a blue streak, aren't I?"

"You're sharing great news. It's fun to hear about. You found someone interested in the antiques, got another part-time job, and were praised by your instructor. I'd say you're on a roll. Before I forget, I was planning to stop by and work for a while tomorrow, but I changed my plans."

"Like I said before, you don't need to come weekends at all."

"I remember but wanted to let you know."

"If you've taken on another job, fine with me. Even with the chaos and mess in this house, staying here awhile longer is better than moving and shelling out money to do it. I'd rather build up my bank account more."

"I hear that. I'm not working another job. When time allows, I work on my own place. It needs my attention."

"You're fixing up your house? Cool."

"I bought a fixer-upper, and making improvements has been challenging due to how busy I am. But it's coming along. I usually do a lot of the work nights and weekends, but this weekend we're celebrating my mom's forty-eighth birthday."

Rose's eyes widened a fraction. "She's an Aquarian too?"

"That's right, your birthdays are both in January." He hadn't thought about that. "Hers is next Monday. Abe's in school and can't make it then. He's driving up from Seattle on Saturday to celebrate."

"Aww, that's sweet." Rose put her hand over the vicinity of her heart. "You and your brother sound like good sons."

"Brandy has always been a real good mom."

"I envy you that. What are you fixing up at your own house?"

"Some of the same stuff I'm doing here. Augie's helping me. Despite being a mess when I bought it, my house has good bones. I've torn out a few walls and replaced a lot of fixtures and appliances that needed updating. Same with the windows and insulation. I cleaned up the yard, too. My neighbors are happy."

"You're a very busy man. Hey, I don't want to be by myself tonight. Do you want to hang out here or go someplace else?"

More than he cared to admit. "Can't—I'm bowling with Buddha."

"Bowling with Buddha. Sounds like a movie title."

"That's his nickname. He's my best bud. His family owns

Gifford Building Supply at the south end of town." He checked his watch. "It's getting late. Save those drawings for another time?"

"I will."

As soon as they both stood, she stepped in close and surprised him with a hug. Not a light one, either. She pressed herself against him. She smelled so good, and her soft curves did a real number on his self-control. His body went haywire. Unlike earlier, he couldn't muster the willpower to pull away. "What are you doing?" he growled, his traitorous arms anchoring her right where she was.

She snuggled into him, breasts to chest, hips to groin. "I feel so close to you."

Way too close. How he wanted her. "This is dangerous," he said, none too friendly as he battled with himself to back away. "We have to stop."

Instead of letting go, she clung to him, her pale green eyes hot with hunger. "Don't you dare tell me I'm vulnerable, Kenny Martin. I'm not. I know what I want—you. Don't fight this. Let it happen."

His rational mind warned him to disentangle himself while he could, but she pressed closer and his mind clouded up. He tilted her head up and kissed her.

CHAPTER 11

Eager for Kenny's kiss, Rose raised up to meet him. His mouth on hers was a new and delicious treat, a brush of softness before he settled in for serious business. "You taste even better than I imagined," he murmured, then kissed her again .

"What did you imagine?" she asked when the second kiss ended, without removing her happy lips from his.

"Nothing as sweet as the real thing." He went back again for more.

Craving something deeper, she licked the seam between his lips. He groaned and slid his tongue into her mouth.

So, so good. She wanted him to touch all her hungry parts —tingling breasts, needy place between her legs. The instant the thought formed, he tore his mouth from hers, gently removed her arms from around him, and stepped back.

"Why did you stop?" she asked, dazed.

"This is wrong."

"It feels right to me."

"I—Let's sit." He moved two of the table chairs next to each other but spaced apart, plunked down and patted the empty seat. As soon as she joined him, he went on. "You say you're not vulnerable, but I don't think you're ready."

"I definitely am. It's been awhile. I'm a twenty-six year old woman with strong physical needs that haven't been met in way too long. Surely you understand that." She couldn't stifle a snicker. "You'd think I'd have figured out Peter was gay. Oh, I suspected he might have someone on the side, but all he did was work and go to conferences. He didn't have time to be with anyone else—or so I told myself. I think he was sexually active when he was away. He went to two conferences a month, claiming he learned a lot. Then there were the times I was gone several times a year."

"Two conferences a month? That's a lot."

Rose agreed. "In hindsight, I don't think he attended half as many. I'm sure he spent a lot of that time having sex with the man he left me for."

"He was a fool to leave you."

"Knowing now that I was the wrong sex and our marriage was a sham, I'm not sorry he did. That doesn't mean I'm not furious over the way he did it." Announcing his plans without any warning or time to process and expecting her to be in charge of the renovations without even asking. Damn him!

"I hope you got tested for STDs," Kenny said.

"I did, and I'm clean. Are you?"

He nodded.

"You already know I signed the papers and sent them off. It shouldn't be long before the divorce is finalized. When I get the notification, I plan to celebrate." She hadn't realized that till she said it.

He seemed to consider the idea, then nodded. "Even with

your uncontested divorce, it could take three to six months to finalize the decree. The length of time is beside the point. I'm not interested in being your rebound romance."

"Who said anything about a romance? Yes, I'm attracted to you, but as I said before, I'm not ready for anything deep and serious. I mean that, Kenny." She looked him straight in the eyes to ensure he believed her.

"So you say, but sex for sex's sake can have unintended consequences, the deep and serious kind you just admitted you're not ready for. There are other ways to take care of your needs."

"I'm aware of that, but—" He brushed her hair back from her face with tenderness, briefly grazing her cheeks with callused fingers, and she forgot the rest of the words. She hadn't noticed the calluses before, but given his work, they made sense. So different from Peter's pristine surgeon's hands. For some reason the imperfection turned her on, made her long to fall back into his arms.

As much as she wanted him, her hot, achy feelings suddenly made her nervous. Maybe Kenny had a point and she wasn't ready for sex after all, especially with him. Not when he was in the house most every day. Bad, bad idea. They were better off as friends. "You're right," she said. "We shouldn't do this."

"Then we're agreed." He checked his watch and stood again. "I have to leave now."

"Bowling awaits—got it." A relief, because she needed to settle down. She decided to spend the evening by herself. "Have a good weekend with your mom."

* * *

SATURDAY MORNING, Kenny slept in. Not as late as he'd hoped, due to an erotic dream featuring Rose. The second one of the night. All hot and bothered, he swore and pushed the hunger away. And cursed himself for giving in and kissing her last night. He was not, *not* getting intimate with her, no matter how much he wanted to. And he really wanted to.

Forcing the thought from his mind, he showered and dressed. He wasn't about to hang around here, pining for what he couldn't have while he waited for Abe and his girl-friend to show up and celebrate their mom's birthday. There were things he needed to do.

After breakfast, he climbed into the truck. It was a clear, cold day, great for his brother's road trip of several hours. Abe was sure to make good time.

Kenny's trip was much shorter. He headed to Gifford's for a load of supplies he'd ordered for the next phase of the remodel. A voice message on his phone the previous evening had notified him the order was in. Originally, he'd planned to relax with his brother and mom today and pick it up Monday morning. Why not now, when he had time? Buddha wasn't in and neither was his father, which was a shame. It would've been good to see one or both of them.

It took a while to get the supplies and load them into the truck. Kenny didn't finish the chore until almost lunchtime. Within minutes of stowing the materials inside the truck top and locking it, the Bluetooth signaled a call from Abe. Smil-ing, he answered, "Morning, little brother. You on your way?"

"Hi, Kenny," said a friendly-sounding female voice. "It's Sedona. I'm calling while Abe drives." Kenny was caught off-guard but didn't mind. "Hey, there. Is my little brother behaving himself?"

"You're on speaker phone," Abe said. "What a ridiculous question. You know I am. I'm younger but not littler—as we're both aware of," he teased. "I'm repeating that for the zillionth time for Sedona."

Kenny chuckled. "What's your ETA?"

"Two hours and change."

"Good to know. I'm about to pick up a sandwich and stuff for the birthday party."

"We're eating ham and cheese sandwiches in the car," Abe said.

Kenny's belly growled. He was hungry himself.

"What are we doing for dinner?"

"You know mom—she wants to cook for us. Sloppy Joes, I think." Abe made a happy sound, and Kenny smiled. "I ordered the cake she always asks for from Melissa Ann's."

"My favorite bakery," Abe said. "My mouth is already watering. Wait'll you taste it, Sedona. It's killer."

"Yum," she said.

"I look forward to meeting you, Sedona," Kenny said before he signed-off.

"Me, too."

Time to get a move-on. A few days ago, he'd contacted a florist in town about putting together a hothouse bouquet of colorful winter flowers. He picked them up, then stopped at the bakery, where the yellow cake with caramel icing she so liked was waiting. Last stop, a gallon of ice cream. After texting his mom to expect him soon, he drove toward her house to wait for Abe and Sedona.

He parked the truck in the guest parking area at his mom's complex. The six-story apartment building was old, but the landlord/owner kept it in reasonable shape.

Brandy had lived there for almost fifteen years and was close to several renters in the building. Gearing up for the visit, he scooped up the cake and flowers and headed for the door. He punched in the numbers and she buzzed him in.

An elevator ride later, he arrived on the fourth floor. Her apartment was halfway down the carpeted hall. The door was open. "Hey, Mom," he called out. All smiles, she came toward him in an apron. "Cooking already?" he said.

"Chopping things for the Sloppy Joes." She eyed the cake box and flowers. "Are those for me?"

"Yup."

"Thank you." She set them down and hugged him. "You're a good son."

Same thing Rose had said shortly before those kisses. Stifling an eye roll at himself, he pulled it together. "You're a great mom. Let's head into the kitchen. You take care of these flowers, and I'll stow the ice cream in the freezer. When Abe phoned a little while ago—correction, Sedona called while he drove—he wondered what we're having for dinner. I told him Sloppy Joes."

Brandy placed her hands on her hips and frowned, reminding him of when he was a kid and misbehaved. "Just how did you know that?"

"It's a favorite of mine and his, that's how."

"Mr. Smart Guy. I bought snacks to nibble on before dinner." She was pretty, and wore her dark brown hair short and sassy. Kenny wished she'd meet someone and have a relationship. "So, Mom, are you dating anyone?"

A mysterious smile bloomed on her face. "As a matter of fact, I am."

He could hardly believe his ears. "No kidding? What's his name?"

"Horace, but everyone calls him 'Racer.' He picked up the name when he ran track in college. He's a customer at the cleaners." She'd worked at the same dry-cleaning place forever. "His wife used to come in all the time till she passed away a few years ago. Anyway, that's how we met."

Kenny wondered how old the guy was. "That's great, Mom. Does he have kids? Where does he work, or is he retired?"

"What is this, the third degree? He has two daughters, one still in high school and the other in college. He's my age, way too young to retire. He's the events manager at the Highway Club. Satisfied now?"

"I don't mean to pry, Mom, but I am curious. Does Abe know about this?"

"Not yet. Tonight, he will."

No doubt he'd be just as surprised. Having been at the club more than a few times for concerts or comedy night, Kenny turned the subject to Racer's job, which was impressive.

"He's doing a great job there," his mom said. "He brings in a lot of class acts. I've seen quite a few." Though they were the only people in the apartment, she leaned in and whispered, "This is top secret, so don't tell anyone. When he can, he gives me a complimentary pass." Then, in a normal voice, "In a little while, you'll meet him. I invited him to join us for dinner."

Whoa. She must really like the guy. Other than an occasional comment from her here and there, Kenny hadn't seen or heard about any adult male since she and Mitchell had divorced. "Have you mentioned Racer before?" he said, working to mask his surprise. Then answered his own question. "I don't think so—I would've remembered the unusual name. This sounds like it could be something serious."

"We're good friends without partners, and we have fun together. That's it. Anything else you want to know, Mr. Nosy?"

"Hey, you're seeing him, you haven't dated at all since your second divorce, and I care about you. That's why I'm asking questions." She'd been single for eleven years and wasn't even fifty. Plenty of time to try again. "You're full of surprises today, Mom. You have a long life ahead. If this thing between you and Racer turns into something serious, I wouldn't object —as long as he's a nice guy and treats you well." He'd know more about the man after they met. "Just sayin.'"

She gave him a fond smile. "I know, and I love you back, Kenny. You should practice what you preach, get out there and meet someone. You're a good-looking man doing well in life, and I'm sure there are lots of available women in town who'd jump at the chance of being with you. Don't you think it's time?" She paused, then added, "For all I know, you already are. You never talk about your social life, either."

Why did his thoughts go to Rose? He knew better, had repeated the reasons why that'd never work to himself multiple times, and added what he'd recently learned—that she didn't want kids. Deal-breaker for him. He wanted them, a minimum of two. Blame his fixation for her on the strong physical pull between them.

He banished her from his thoughts. "I put new windows in the house. Come over sometime and see it." Then he gestured toward the kitchen. "It's great that you decided to cook for your birthday, but the last thing I want is to sit around and twiddle my thumbs while we wait for everybody. It's your birthday celebration, so why don't you put me to work and sit down?"

"You don't want to talk about your love life with your mother—I understand. I don't want to sit right now, okay? But I'll take you up on the offer of help. While we're getting everything ready, tell me about your latest project and anything else you're up to. Hint, hint."

Kenny stuck to his current job, telling her about the doctor who'd hired him and moved to another state, the renovation, and how he'd dropped the divorce on Rose the very day he'd caught a flight out.

"What a terrible way to deliver that news," Brandy said. "He sounds like an awful man."

"I only spent about an hour and a half, total, with him, and I couldn't say except for what he did to Rose. At first she was in shock, but she seems to be doing pretty well." He filled Brandy in about the interior design program.

"I've never known anyone in that field. Hmm," she said and gave him a speculative frown.

"Why are you looking at me like that?" Kenny asked.

"Like what? The husband sounds like a jerk, but the job sounds like a good one. I'll bet Rose is glad you're around."

"I wouldn't know about that. The team and I don't see much of her." He'd stretched the truth, to keep her from getting any ideas. Kenny asked her about her job, which got her talking about herself instead of speculating about him. As soon as they finished with the cooking stuff, he set the table.

Then Abe and Sedona arrived, and his mom diverted her attention there.

CHAPTER 12

Hours later, after Kenny's mom opened her gifts—Abe's coupon for free yard service whenever he was home, a small box of chocolates from Sedona, which was real nice of her, a pretty scarf from Racer, and Kenny's check to spend wherever and however she wanted—the group settled in to enjoy their cake and ice cream.

Racer seemed like a decent guy. Tall and wiry like the runner he still was, he was friendly and cracked corny dad jokes that had people rolling their eyes. The way he looked at Brandy made his feelings obvious. He really liked her. She seemed to like him, too. Good friends, my foot. They were closer than that. Time would tell what happened with them.

Sedona was great, too, warm and friendly. She and Abe made an interesting couple—him tall and lanky, her a little slip of a person, the top of her head a few inches shy of reaching his shoulder. Smart, too, and strong. A good match for his kid brother.

Wanting to get Brandy's opinion of her, Kenny followed

her down the hallway toward the bathroom and conferred with her in a low voice. "What do you think of Sedona?"

"I like her a lot."

"Me, too. Racer seems like a good guy. That scarf he bought you is really pretty."

She smiled and touched her neck, where she'd tied it. "Sky blue is a great color on me. I might use the cash you gave me to find a pretty dress to wear with it." She raised up and kissed her cheek. "It's way too generous."

"You're my mom. You deserve it." He left her and headed into the kitchen where Abe, Sedona, and Racer were cleaning up the dinner and dessert mess.

When they finished, it was still early yet. Sedona suggested they play charades. They had a lot of fun, competing against each other and laughing. In the end, Sedona won.

Although Kenny had a great time, he couldn't help but envy his brother and his mother with their partners. The looks they shared, two couples on the verge of something that could become serious. He was the lone man out. Not for long, if he could help it. As soon as he got home tonight, he'd sign up for several dating apps. Maybe he'd get lucky and meet the person he was looking for. He stubbornly steered his thoughts away from Rose, yet they hovered in the back of his mind.

* * *

WORKING three days in a row at Panache turned out to be harder than Rose had imagined. By the time she closed up shop and went home late Sunday afternoon, she was utterly exhausted. She hadn't touched the iPad or thought about Kenny all weekend. Which wasn't quite true. She'd thought about his potent kisses and how good it'd felt holding onto him and being held in return. And here she was, fantasizing once more.

What had gotten into her? It was a good thing they'd agreed to steer clear of doing anything like that again, no matter how much she'd enjoyed herself or craved more. Sex with anyone right now was a bad idea, and she was grateful he'd stopped things from going any further. Maybe she'd stay away from the house while he was there. That way, she wouldn't get into trouble.

For dinner she mixed beaten eggs with shredded cheese and cooked the meal in the microwave. Ugh—lately her standard reaction—but better than nothing. While she ate, she thought about Vi. Her sister and Blake had arrived home earlier. The food revived her energy level enough to send a text. *Welcome home! Can't wait to talk! Too tired now and about to fall into bed super early .I worked all weekend. Tell you about that later. Love you and Blake both. Nighty night.*

After silencing her phone, she fell into a deep sleep. She didn't stir until the morning alarm pinged her awake. Shortly after she checked her messages, she found one from Vi saying she was equally tired, and another from Kenny. He was arriving earlier than usual, some forty minutes from now.

The thought of seeing him made her both uncomfortable and way too eager. Hoping to avoid him, at least this morning, she started a pot of coffee for herself and him and his crew, then quickly showered, dressed, and ate a quick bowl of cereal.

After pouring some of the coffee in a to-go cup, she headed for the coat closet. She was about to get her coat when a knock sounded at the door. Kenny had arrived.

CHAPTER 13

Out of politeness and because Rose was still home at seven-thirty Monday morning, Kenny knocked on the door rather than let himself in. She opened it holding a to-go coffee cup in her hand. The top of her iPad peeked from her purse. Every time he saw her, his day brightened considerably. "Mornin,'" he greeted cheerfully.

"Morning," she answered with a lackluster smile.

Okay, then. He was still glad to see her even if the smile wasn't as bright as he'd grown to expect.

"You didn't use the key," she commented.

"I knew you were here and figured you'd let me in." While he explained, she set her things down and opened the coat closet.

She seemed in a big hurry with no sign of the enthusiasm he'd noted the previous week. Her class didn't start for almost an hour. Maybe she had breakfast plans out. Disappointing—he'd wanted to talk for a little while and compare weekends. Wherever she was off to wasn't his business. Regardless, he had to ask. "Do you have a meeting this morning?"

She shook her head. "Things to do. FYI, I'm going to be super busy for a while and won't be home much."

Which would take care of the temptation problem. "Okay." He set his tool kit down to help her into her coat. Caught a whiff of the light, sweet scent that was becoming familiar. Much as he'd tried, he hadn't stopped thinking about her all weekend. Good thing he'd pulled himself together this morning and wouldn't see much of her anymore.

"I don't need your help with my coat, but thanks," she said.

In a rush and prickly, too. "No problem." Except it was. His body hadn't gotten the message to behave. At times, he was a real dog. He steered his gaze away from that tempting mouth and stepped back. "I haven't forgotten about the antique dealer coming this afternoon. The crew and I should leave around four so we won't get in the way. If you're not back by then, I'll leave you a note about what was done today to share with Peter."

"I'd appreciate that. Cross your fingers the dealer offers to rep a whole bunch of stuff."

"He may not buy it outright," Kenny warned. "A lot of businesses opt to sell the pieces on consignment."

"What exactly does that mean?" Rose asked.

"If they sell, you get money. What doesn't sell goes back to you."

"I never realized, and I never thought to ask." She yawned.

Noting the shadows under her eyes he'd missed due to his focus on her lips, he understood the reason for her ho-hum greeting. She was exhausted. "Rough weekend, huh?"

"You have no idea. I'm not used to working three days in a row at Panache and had no clue the job was so taxing. I sound like a total lightweight. I didn't used to be, but with Peter supporting me since we moved in together almost three years ago, I've become one.

"But how could I possibly know what it'd be like to be there such long hours? Before meeting Peter, I worked at the hospital gift shop. Easy peasy. After I moved in with him, I worked a four-hour shift at Panache once a week, for extra spending money. He was generous on birthdays and holidays and paying for my clothes, hair appointments, and so on, which was great, but he wasn't so good about the little everyday things I needed. As much as I love the clothes Panache carries, working at a women's boutique isn't nearly as fun as the internship. Good God, I'm rambling on again."

Not minding at all, he smiled. "Too bad you can't work more hours at the internship instead."

"Wouldn't that be nice. I'm lucky to be there at all. I'll get used to the hours at Panache—I don't have much choice. I made coffee if you want it. How was your mom's birthday party?"

"I thought you were in a hurry to leave."

"I can wait a little longer. Tell me quickly."

"We had a good time. I met my brother's girlfriend, and found out my mother's dating someone."

"Sounds interesting. I—"

The ringing doorbell announcing the arrival of the crew stifled whatever she'd started to say. Rose greeted them, repeated the coffee offer, and left.

* * *

AFTER CLASS THAT MORNING, Rose stayed on campus and spent hours in the quiet of the library designing imaginary rooms on the iPad. The exhaustion from the weekend faded, worries and problems vanished, and all felt right in the world. Amazing how letting her creativity out invigorated her. To the point that she vowed to make time to use it even if she was overwhelmed after shifts at Panache.

To her surprise, hours had passed. She needed to get home right away and prep for Bill Robie's visit.

Kenny would enjoy the drawings she'd made, but he'd be gone when she got home. Having said this morning that she wouldn't be around much for her own good had been the right thing to do, but already she missed him. She wanted to find out more about his mother and brother and the people they were seeing, and otherwise catch up. How had seeing and talking to him become a habit?

She found the notes for Peter and pocketed them. Starving hungry, she grabbed a can of peanuts, which she nibbled while she double-checked the list of antiques she'd compiled. She revisited each room to make sure she hadn't missed anything. Then, thanking the gods for the printer Peter had left behind, she made a copy of it for Bill Robie. And decided she'd take the printer with her when she moved.

Shortly after five, Mr. Robie rang the doorbell. "I brought Ron along," he said once inside. "He's my nephew and assistant and is learning about the business. This is Rose Shafer."

"Hi," she said, taking their coats. "Excuse the mess. My soon-to-be ex-husband took the furniture and pieces he wanted and left the rest. He also decided to have some renovations done."

The dealer raised his eyebrows. "And you get to keep what's here?"

"That's what he said." She handed over the list. "Here are all the pieces considered to be antiques." Or so Peter had told her soon after they married. "I can print out a duplicate for Ron."

"We'll share."

After glancing at the list and conferring softly with his nephew, who listened carefully, he nodded. "We want to see everything you're selling."

Rose wondered about the consignment policy. "Will this be a consignment deal, or do you pay up front?"

"Good question. That depends on the quality, the market, and other things. I'll let you know after we look at everything."

Bill had a keen eye and fired off notes that Ron dutifully jotted down. After finishing and conferring with his nephew, he opted to buy almost everything outright. Rose was thrilled, but managed to keep her cool. While Ron carefully packed each piece to avoid damage, his boss wrote her a check that made her eyes widen. That much? She barely contained her amazement.

Ron went outside to the Robie Antiques van they'd arrived in and returned with a hand truck. The two men loaded the items and transported them to the van. Three trips for the heavier things and another for the smaller pieces.

Rose waited until the van had rolled out of the driveway before she raised her hands and shouted, "Yahoo!" right there in the living room.

She thought about depositing the check right away, but first things first. She called Kenny with the news. Had to. "It's me, Rose. I hope I'm not bothering you."

"Hi, there," he said, sounding pleased to hear from her. "I

was about to get dinner, but that can wait. I'm thinking you have good news?"

"You think right," she said, smiling even though he couldn't see her. "Bill Robie, the antique guy, just left."

"It's nearly seven o'clock. Either he arrived late, or he spent a lot of time looking at the pieces you want to get rid of."

Had he been there that long? She should've been hungry but due to excitement hadn't been. Now though, the mere thought had her stomach rumbling. "He was on time, but there was a lot to look at and evaluate. Also, he brought his nephew, an antique beginner wanting to learn the ropes, and it all took a while. Guess what? He ended up buying every-thing except a little table that'd been refinished with enamel paint, which reduced its value to almost nothing. He didn't take anything on consignment, he paid up front!" She couldn't hold back a squeal of delight.

Kenny chuckled. "That *is* good news. I hope he gave you what they're worth."

"I wouldn't know, but it's a lot, enough to really fatten my bank account. I'm going to do the same thing with other furniture I don't want—as soon as I find a company willing to sell it. That or put an ad on Craigslist."

"Good ideas."

"Right? I have Peter to thank for this. Not that I'm going to tell him anything." If he ever found out… She didn't want him asking for some of the money. Besides, he didn't deserve to know. He'd told her to do what she wanted with what he'd left behind, and she had. "You can't imagine how excited I am."

"As a matter of fact, your voice gave you away," he said, sounding as if he was grinning.

"The same way I know you're smiling." It was a good thing

he wasn't there or she'd throw her arms around him. Make herself ache for him? Bad idea. Better one: deposit the check, then celebrate with a chocolaty treat from Melissa Ann's Bakery. She was already salivating. "I should go. Thanks for rooting for me and letting me share the news."

"Thanks for telling me. Before we disconnect, did you see the note about the work my team and I did today?"

"Yes, and I'll text Peter later. Have a good evening."

After eating a cheese sandwich, she left the house. And smiled all the way to the bank.

CHAPTER 14

A week later after class, still giddy to be flush with money of her own for the first time ever, Rose decided to look for a place to live. She drove around the south end of town where things weren't as posh as where she was now to search for places with For Rent signs, in particular a house with other tenants looking for another person to split the rent. She saw plenty of nice homes but not a single rental notice. What a disappointment. May as well explore a few more side streets in the area before she gave up and headed home.

She drove down several with no luck. One last street, then she'd call it quits for now. Marigold Avenue, the street sign said. A two-lane road in an area of small yards and modest homes. Three-quarters of the way down, she saw the sign she'd been hoping to find. At last.

The two-story house was a pretty blue-gray with white trim. So well-kept, it had to be for a single family. The rent was bound to be way more than she could afford, but it couldn't hurt to find out. She parked out front, then crossed the blacktop driveway and headed for the door.

Seconds after walking across the front stoop and pressing the doorbell, she heard the thud of footsteps. The woman who opened the door had short, salt and pepper hair. "Hello," she said with a welcoming smile. "Are you here to see the apartment?"

Apartment? That didn't make sense, but Rose played along. "I happened to be driving by and saw the sign. I'd love to see it. I'm Rose Shafer."

"Barb Simon. Would you believe Jerome and I just put the sign up half an hour ago? The apartment entrance is around to the side. Come inside where it's warm while I get the key. Then I'll take you up."

From Rose's vantage point in the entry, she could see the living room, an uncluttered space with an off-white and sage green patterned rug over an oak floor. There was a fireplace, too, and furniture that looked comfortable and inviting. She was already in love with the house and hadn't even glimpsed the apartment.

Seconds later Barb returned, key in hand. "Follow me," she said, then continued talking as they headed to the far side of the house. "Tell me about yourself, Rose."

"I'm twenty-six and soon to be divorced. I'll be graduating from Port Simms Community College in March, and I need a place to live."

Barb nodded and stopped at what was apparently the outside entrance to the apartment. She unlocked the door. "It's just up the stairs."

The carpeted staircase led up to another door, this one to

the apartment. "So it's upstairs," Rose said. "Has it always been an apartment?"

"As far as we know. It was this way when we bought it six years ago after our kids were out of the nest for good and we decided to downsize. We've been renting it out ever since. We're partial to students. In our experience, they tend to be quieter. It's a small one-bedroom, fully furnished." She unlocked the door and gestured Rose inside. "Take a look around."

Due to the size of the place, that didn't take long. A living room about as big as the den at Peter's, a compact kitchen with a table big enough to seat at most four, standard bathroom, modest bedroom. The bedroom closet was surprisingly big. With so much space for storage and clothes, who cared how small the rest of the place was? "It's perfect," Rose said, crossing her fingers that she could afford it.

Barb broke into a smile. "I'm so glad you like it. I assume you want to know the rent and what it covers."

While she went over the details, Rose caught her breath and waited to find out the monthly rent. The landlady quoted an amount so reasonable and affordable, she could hardly believe her ears. There must be a catch. Maybe she should check the ratings first. But a place like this was sure to be snatched up in no time. Common sense urged her to find out.

Dealing with Peter had taught her to think fast. "The rent seems low for such a nice place," she said.

"On purpose. Jerome and I believe if we take care of our tenant, she or he will take care of the apartment. To be on the safe side, though, we ask for higher damage and cleaning deposits. If you leave the unit in good condition, you'll get the damage deposit back."

That sounded reasonable. Still, needing a moment, Rose asked to use the bathroom. Once closeted in there, she googled the address and checked for reviews. She didn't find anything, but this wasn't exactly a run-of-the-mill rental. Regardless, the deal was too good to pass up. She decided to take a chance.

A short time later, after Barb introduced her to Jerome, a balding man with twinkling eyes, they sat down over coffee and conversation. The landlords wanted to know how she planned to pay the rent. She told them about her two part-time jobs and shared her dream of working full time at Thompson's when she graduated. Then it was Rose's turn for questions, all of which they answered to her satisfaction.

She agreed to move in on a Saturday a few weeks from now—provided her boss gave the okay to take that day off, fingers crossed—and signed a six-month lease with an option to extend if both parties were in agreement. After the land-lords signed and Jerome went somewhere in the house to make a copy for him and Barb, Rose wrote a check for the deposits and first month's rent.

The deal was done. The searching, finding, and signing had taken awhile, and by the time she left darkness had fallen. Exhilarated, she started the car and let it idle. Living by herself would be quite an adjustment, but if she didn't like it, well, six months wasn't that long.

She wanted to tell everyone right away, both friends and family, Kenny included, although she'd avoided him for a whole week, mainly to curtail her feelings. First, she needed food. Why not buy herself dinner for once—takeout, as she didn't like to eat alone in public. Still sitting in the car outside her home-to-be, she called Pinole's, a pizzeria known for its wood-fired oven that wasn't too far from her newfound home. She ordered a pizza big enough to last several nights. What a shame living on the east side meant it'd take a while to get home, but the yummy pie she wanted more than made up for the twenty-minute drive. Thin crust, savory toppings… Her mouth was already watering.

Being a Monday night and past the usual dinner hour, traffic was light. She arrived earlier than planned. The parking lot wasn't near full. She approached the lone person behind the counter, a woman with jet black hair tied back who looked to be in her late thirties or early forties. "Hi," she said. "I'm Rose Shafer here to pick up my order."

"Nice to meet you, Rose," the woman said with a friendly smile. "I'm Maria. Your order isn't ready yet, but should be soon. We're not busy tonight. Feel free to sit at an empty table while you wait."

About half the tables were occupied. Rose found a booth and shrugged out of her coat. While she waited, she texted Gran, Vi, and her friends the good news about the antiques. She didn't mention the apartment, which was sure to lead to questions about what she'd found, due to being too hungry to deal with that just yet. As she finished, the sudden blast of cold air that blew in told her that someone had exited or entered the pizzeria.

"Hey," a familiar voice called out.

Kenny. Missing him more than she'd admitted to herself, she turned her head his way. Seeing him was a treat in itself, and she drank in the sight. Big and good-looking to begin with, the faded jeans that hinted at his muscular legs, Mizzle ankle boots—she knew fashion and recognized the merino wool, water repellent boots—and a well-worn leather jacket gave him a rugged, powerful, air. He oozed style and sex appeal. Mr. Hot.

Add in his grin and he was impossible to turn away from. Hoo boy. Her heart thudded and her stomach fluttered. She wasn't the only entranced female in the room. Several of them openly checked him out. "What are you doing here?" she asked.

"Same thing as you, getting myself a pizza. Is this seat taken?" Without waiting for an answer, he sat down across from her.

Now all eyes were on the pair of them. Envious, she imagined. *Eat your hearts out, ladies.* As soon as the thought entered her mind, she banished it. She and Kenny weren't involved, and she had no hold on him. "FYI, I won't be sitting here long. I ordered mine to-go and am waiting for it."

"You're pretty far from where you live. Why drive all the way to the south side just to pick up a pizza?"

She couldn't believe he'd asked. She snorted. "This isn't any old pizza. It's the best pizza in town, that's why. Plus, I'm celebrating. I just rented an apartment."

"Yeah? Where?"

"About a ten-minute drive from here."

"Huh. I'm about fifteen minutes away, on Crescent Avenue." He shrugged out of his jacket and set it beside him on the booth. The dark green color of his flannel shirt brought out the gold tones of his eyes. "I also pre-ordered, but for here. Where is this apartment you rented?"

May as well tell him now, even if she was beyond hungry. "Marigold Avenue. I was driving around, looking for places to rent, and there it was!" She told him about the house with the little apartment above it. "I had no idea you lived around here."

"I bought the place after the divorce. We're almost neighbors, or will be. When do you move?"

"About that. I signed a lease that starts February fifteenth. If you're not done with the house by then, I'll pop in regularly to check your progress."

"Or you can trust me."

"I do, but Peter paid me a bundle to watch over things. I really shouldn't be here—Vi is taking me out tomorrow night for at late birthday celebration, but now that I have a bigger bank balance, I decided to treat myself. Shouldn't you tell someone here you've arrived?"

"Nah. They know me—I come in all the time." He waved at Maria, busy boxing pizzas for other to-go orders. "Hey, Maria."

"Hey, Kenny," she returned. "Your pie will be ready soon. Yours is ready now, Rose."

As she stood to get it, he reached out his hand and stopped her. Instant bolt of excitement throughout her body. She pulled out of his grasp. He looked stricken. "Sorry about that. I wasn't thinking. I was about to say you should stay and eat here while the food's hot. I'd appreciate the company. That's all, I swear. No touching, just a meal between friends."

A tempting offer to a starving woman. Should she or shouldn't she? "I guess I could do that."

His expression blanked. "If you don't want to, that's okay."

Oh, she wanted to, in the worst way. Wanted him, period, even if it was a bad idea. If she made sure to keep the urge and her hands to herself and simply take him at his word that they were friends eating together, everything should be okay. "No, it's a good idea. I'll be right back." At the counter she told Maria she'd decided to eat there with Kenny and ordered herself a pop. After paying, she attempted to carry the pizza and her drink at the same time.

"Go sit down," Maria said. "I'll bring everything to you and save the box for your leftovers."

Within moments, there were two plates, silverware, napkins, and drinks at the table. Rose gaped at the server. "I didn't order Kenny anything to drink because I wasn't sure what he wanted. How did you know what to bring?"

He flashed a smile at the server. "Like I said, Maria knows me."

The woman gave him the same friendly smile she'd given Rose. "He likes on-tap beer with his pizza. He's been eating here since we first opened, haven't you, Kenny?"

"Sure have. No other pizza compares. Plus, it's minutes from my house." When Maria left, he raised his beer. "To you for finding yourself a place to move."

"Thanks, Kenny. Cheers."

"Which pizza did you order?" he asked.

"The one with pears and Gorgonzola cheese and thin crust. It's amazing. You?"

"Olives, sausage, green pepper, onions, cheese, and chicken, also on thin crust."

"Two meats? That's a loaded pizza. "

"The way I like it."

"Where I am now, restaurants are few and far between. Such a shame. "

"It's an upscale neighborhood. This is blue-collar country."

Maria delivered both pizzas at the same time, along with salads. Rose had never eaten a meal with Kenny. He was hungry and wolfed down the first slice within minutes. "You make that pizza look so good," she said.

"It is. Yours looks tasty, too. I've tried almost everything on the menu here, but not that one. Let's swap slices."

They did and tried each other's orders. "Yours is delicious," she said. "I might have to get one for myself next time."

Busy chewing a bite of the slice she'd given him, he didn't reply. He seemed to enjoy it as much as she did his. "I could get seriously addicted to this place, which could be dangerous to my waistline," she said when they began to slow down. "I thought sure I'd need a roommate to help pay the rent, but with what they're charging me, I don't." She made a face. "I've never lived alone, though. My friend, Pressley, swears by solo living."

"I don't mind, either. You get used to it."

"I'll find out, won't I? I guess if I feel lonely, I'll go out."

"You can always call me." He linked his gaze with hers, as if he could see right into her soul.

Nervous, she glanced at the napkin on her lap. "Tell me about your mom's birthday."

"She turned forty-eight."

"Happy Birthday, Kenny's mom. I meant the party a week or so back. You said something about her dating. You met the guy, right?"

"Horace, but he goes by Racer. He seems nice and really likes my mom. Has a great job, too, lining up acts at the Highway Club."

"I used to go to that club. I haven't been in ages, since before I met Peter."

"That's a long time."

She shrugged. "He wasn't interested, and when he was out

of town, I usually had plans somewhere else." The mere mention of her soon-to-be ex gave her a bad taste, and she steered the conversation back to the birthday party. "You were talking about Racer and your mother."

"Right. It was nice to see her interested in someone. She hasn't dated since the divorce, at least not that she's said." He shook his head. "But then, I don't talk about my social life, either."

He must be dating. Dying to know, she angled him a look. "Who did you bring to the party?"

"I'm not dating anyone now, but I'm working on that."

Rose didn't want him to be looking for someone, which was ridiculous. She had no right to care, had been doing her best to avoid him. Which was exactly what she'd told herself when he'd first joined her in the booth. "The way I feel, I can't even think about dating," she said, which was the truth.

"That makes sense. It's too soon, and you have a lot on your plate."

"I really do." But she sure had thoughts about being with Kenny. Thoughts she fought to hide. Time to go home before she did something she'd regret. She made a show of checking her watch. "It's getting late and I have to be up early. So do you." She signaled Maria to bring her the check and the pizza box.

Kenny did the same. Maria brought the boxes and the bills. He paid both on his credit card. Not wanting the evening to feel like a date, Rose paid him back in cash. When Maria returned with the credit slip for him to sign, she cast a smile at both of them. "You two make a beautiful couple."

"We're not together—" she and Kenny said in unison.

"Okay. Have a good night." As the server returned, she murmured what sounded like, "Maybe you should be."

"Did you hear what I heard?" Rose asked.

"I sure did. Maria has never been subtle. Let's go."

Coats on and pizza boxes in hand, they exited the pizzeria. After the warmth inside the building Rose shivered in the cold night air. She and Kenny headed in the same direction. As it turned out, he'd parked the next row over from hers.

"Give me that box," he said.

"I was about to set it on the roof of the car, but okay." She handed it over and unlocked the door. He set her box on the passenger seat.

"I enjoyed tonight, Rose."

"Me, too. Their gazes locked, easy to see in the bright perimeter lights. If ever there was a perfect moment to kiss each other… Wanting /not wanting that, she glanced down at her key fob. It was a good thing his arms were full with his own pizza box.

"Hey, do you want to see my apartment?" she asked, not quite ready for the evening to end. "We can't go in, but there's no reason why we shouldn't drive by. Follow me there, and then we'll go on our separate ways."

"Sure. I'd like that."

Relieved to be in different cars, which would keep them out of temptation's way, she slid into the driver's seat. As always, she pressed the starter button. Nothing happened, not then and not for the next two tries. Kenny was backing his truck out of the slot. She hurried over to it and knocked on the window. "Kenny?"

He rolled it down. "Yeah?"

"My car won't start. I tried several times and nothing."

"Maybe you flooded it."

"I don't think so. It never turned over."

"Hang on." He pulled back into the slot, parked, and exited the truck.

* * *

KENNY HAD NEVER REALLY LOOKED at Rose's car. No reason to. He did now. "Is that a 2015 Camry?"

"How did you know? Let me guess—besides being a primo renovations guy you're also a car fanatic?"

He laughed. "Primo renovations, huh? I like that. I'm no car expert, but I do know a few things. I recognize your car because Augie drives the same model and year."

"Has he had problems with his?"

"Not that I know of." Kenny had a problem, though. A big one. His attraction to Rose was killing him. Those big, green eyes that were impossible not to fall into. He'd managed to curb his desire while they ate, but when they exited to the parking lot and their eyes had locked... The longing on her face had stirred his hunger to a fever pitch, and he'd almost lost control of himself. Thanks to a firm grip on his willpower, he'd managed to subdue the intense feelings that seemed to grow each time he was with her.

Getting in the truck to go home had been a relief. But now, he was in big trouble.

"—hadn't either," she commented, and he realized he'd missed whatever she'd been saying. "I bought mine in 2020 from an elderly man who'd given up driving. He'd only put twenty-thousand miles on it, and the mechanic Vi suggested I hire to check it out gave it a thumbs-up. It's been a great car and never given me a moment's problem until tonight. I have no idea why it won't start."

"I'll take a look. Hand me the key." He was totally focused on the car and not the woman who'd moved to the passenger side. In the driver's seat, he attempted to start the engine. As she'd said, it didn't even try to turn over. He could think of several reasons for that. "How much gas is in the car?"

"More than half a tank."

"Have you had trouble starting it before?"

"Once or twice, but it's always started."

"Did you add antifreeze this year?"

"I always left that stuff up to Peter. He may have taken care of it, but I'm certainly not going to call him and ask. Why?"

"Because it's winter and you don't want any engine parts to freeze."

Her eyes widened. "I've never considered doing that. Tonight's cold, but not that cold. It rarely is."

"True. How's the battery?"

"Fine, I guess."

She guessed? "When was the last time you took the car in for servicing?"

"I don't remember—it's been awhile." She gave him a blank look. "I've never had any problems. Why, am I supposed to take it in periodically?"

"Most people get it checked every now and then for a tune-up and oil change. That's usually when the mechanics let you know about the health of your battery. The info for your car should be in the booklet that came with it."

"What booklet? I never got one."

"I'm not surprised. The previous owner probably lost it. Your mechanic would know—if you have one. I'm guessing you don't." She shrugged. "Peter never said anything about that?"

"To tell you the truth, we never discussed our vehicles." She put her forehead in her hands and groaned. "I hope I haven't ruined my car."

"Doubtful. My guess is on the battery. I'll try to jumpstart it. Do you have jumper cables?"

"As I've never needed them, I don't."

"Are you sure? Have you checked the trunk?"

She rolled her eyes. "If I did, I'd know. There's nothing in there but a spare tire and tools for if I get a flat. Now what?"

"I have a pair in the truck. Hang on, and I'll grab them." He retrieved his set and returned. No longer in the passenger seat, she stood near the car, her hands in the pockets of her coat. He raised the hood of the truck, then paused. "Why don't I teach you how to hook up and use the cables. In case you ever need to do it."

Her eyebrows rose, as if the idea surprised her. "Okay."

She was beside him as he coached her to hook up the truck. Her hair smelled good. He wanted to nuzzle her neck, kiss the tender place below her earlobe. Instead, after he hooked up the truck, he directed her through the same exercise on the Camry. "Congratulations," he said. "You did it."

"I did, didn't I?" She beamed at him. "It's not at all hard to do. Now what?"

"Sit in the driver's seat of the Camry. Don't try to turn it on until I tell you, and don't accelerate." She nodded, and he went on. "I'm going to start the truck now. I'll holler when it's time for you to start yours." It didn't take long before she was able to start her car. Don't turn it off," he counseled. "Let it run. It helps the battery charge."

"I will. I'm so glad I ran into you here."

"Funny the way things work out. Sometime soon you should get the battery checked to see if it needs replacing. You should also get a tune-up in the near future."

"That could be expensive. I might put it off for a while."

"I wouldn't. At the very least, you'll find out if there's anything else wrong with it. No matter what you decide about the tune-up, get the battery checked. You might also want to get yourself some cables."

"I'll do both when I have time."

"Any mechanic can install a new battery. If you belong to Triple A, call them. They'll come out and take care of it at your house or wherever you are."

"Peter has a membership, but I don't have the account number. I guess I could call the company and try to get it. Technically, we are still married. In the meantime, I need to get home. I guess I won't be showing you where my apartment is tonight."

"Another time."

"Cross your fingers the car starts in the morning."

He felt for her. "If it doesn't, contact Triple A right away and get on the schedule. Like I said, someone will come to wherever the car is and take care of it. Including your house. If they can't rush right over, I'll give you a lift to work."

With so much still left to do at the house, he couldn't believe he'd offered.

"No, Kenny. You've done enough. If I need to, I'll call Lyft for a ride." She fiddled with her hair. "What if the car dies while I'm on the way home tonight?"

"Keep it running, and you'll get there just fine." It was

growing later by the minute. He wanted to go home, get some sleep, and not think about her anymore. He turned to leave.

"Wait," Rose said, and opened the door of her Camry. "Don't worry, I'm leaving the motor on." She exited, moved closer to him, and clasped his hands in hers.

"Damn, your hands are cold. What are you doing?"

"Yours are a lot warmer than mine. I know we agreed not to touch or kiss, and I promise this will be short and basically harmless." She lifted his hands and planted multiple kisses on the knuckles of each. "Thank you, Kenny, for having dinner with me and helping with my car."

He was so startled by the feel of those soft lips on his skin and so touched, he couldn't speak for a moment. When she let go and stepped back, his voice returned. "You're welcome."

CHAPTER 15

The following morning, Rose woke up early despite tossing and turning and pining for Kenny. She had things to do before leaving for the internship. First, shower and dress. Next, find out if the car started. If it didn't, find Peter's Triple A number and request that someone stop by the house and install a new battery. She wasn't about to take a chance on the thing dying again.

She also needed to order a Lyft to drive her to Thompson's, then text her family and friends about the apartment and the move-in date. If she kept herself nice and busy, she wouldn't think too much about her growing need to be with Kenny. Each time she was with him, the hunger grew by leaps.

Maybe she was ready for sex after all, but now was no time to angst over that.

The car failed to start, darn it. She managed to find an old Triple A renewal reminder in the back of the mostly empty top drawer of the desk Peter had left behind. Did they change the membership numbers from year to year, and had Peter renewed the membership? She had no idea, but was about to find out.

Crossing her fingers that the company was open this early, she called. Luckily, a woman answered. Even better, when she supplied the membership number it was accepted. She explained the situation and requested that someone come to the house and replace the battery while she was at work.

The woman scheduled the appointment for mid-morning. Rose gave Kenny's name as the person who'd be there, crossing her fingers he wouldn't mind letting them into the garage and giving them the check. When she asked about the cost, the woman on the phone couldn't give her the exact amount. Apparently, that depended on the kind of battery. More than one kind? Who knew?

She felt dumb for knowing so little about her own car and neglecting to have it serviced once in a while when Peter was still around to pay the bill. Also for letting others do things for her during the past three years that most people did them-selves. That was going to change.

After checking her watch to make sure she had enough time to order a Lyft that would deliver her to Thompson's on time, she signed a blank check, which probably wasn't smart. Good thing she trusted Kenny. She stuck it in the same desk drawer where she'd found the old Triple A reminder. She should probably give him something for his trouble but doubted he'd take money from her. Hmm. Maybe a treat from Melissa Ann's. Last, she ordered the Lyft to pick her up in thirty minutes.

Then, feeling good and congratulating herself for jobs well done, she brewed a pot of coffee and nuked several slices of last night's pizza for breakfast. Microwaving didn't hurt the taste at all. It was almost as good as freshly baked.

She was brushing her teeth and touching up her lip gloss when Kenny texted. He was running late. She'd been hoping to explain about the battery person coming to the house. She phoned him instead.

"Rose?" he answered.

The frown in his voice put her off. "Sorry to bother you," she started. "I need to fill you in on a few things."

"Let me guess—the car didn't start and you want a ride."

"You're right, it didn't start. It's a good thing I made it home without any problem."

"If I'd thought otherwise, I'd have followed you there."

Of course, he would've. He was that kind of man, ready to help when asked, and knowing so warmed her heart. "I know, and I appreciate your help last night. I don't need a ride. I've already ordered and prepaid Lyft. But I do have a favor to ask." She explained the situation and the battery person's ETA. "When they come, would you mind opening the garage door and later paying them? I signed a check and filled in the date, but I left the amount blank. The check is in the top desk drawer in the office. If you could fill in the amount, I—" she paused, wondering how to thank him. "There's a reward for you."

"Oh, yeah? Gonna kiss my knuckles again?"

Apparently, that hadn't gone over well. She deflated a little. "It was a spur of the moment thing. Weird, I know, but not suggestive, right? I had no idea I was going to do it until I did. I swear, it won't happen again."

"I thought it was sweet."

Phew. She relaxed and smiled. The phoned beeped with a

text from the ride she'd ordered. "I should go—the Lyft driver will be here in five minutes." She still needed to gather up her things.

"Hey, tell your sister and Blake congrats from me. Before we disconnect, will you need a ride home?"

"I won't, thanks," she said as she headed for the fridge in the dining room and put two more pizza slices into a food container with a lid. A lot of pizza today, but she was in a rush. "This is the night Vi takes me out for a birthday dinner, and we have a lot to catch up on." She noted the car pulling up the driveway. "My ride is here. Talk to you later. Thanks in advance for helping me out with the battery person. Text if you need to." She hustled outside.

* * *

AT THE END of the workday, Kenny met Buddha at the bowling alley for a couple of games followed by bowling alley food, which was no great shakes but a long-held tradition they enjoyed. After the one previous game a few weeks earlier they both were still rusty, but they had a good time. "I trounced you the second game," he crowed over hotdogs and fries.

Buddha snorted. "Only because I was tired after beating the socks off you the first game."

They bantered back and forth and made small talk. Fine with Kenny. He didn't want to get into anything too personal, like his growing feelings for Rose. So far tonight, he hadn't thought about her at all and wanted to keep it that way.

Then his cell rang—a call from her. "I have to take this," he said and stood to move out of eavesdropping range. "Hey," he answered. "Aren't you supposed to be having dinner with your sister?"

"Good news—the new battery works! I got a Lyft to the house and drove myself to the restaurant, and I'm waiting for her now. Where are you? Sounds like bowling."

"You guessed it. Buddha and I played a few games. Now we're eating. Where are you having dinner?"

"Sweet Sue's."

"Classy place to eat." Pricey, too.

"Vi can afford it. When her birthday comes around, I'll treat her, but depending on work, nothing that expensive. Forget I said that. She's worth the splurge. It's what we do for each other, just the two of us. I won't keep you. I wanted to thank you again for helping me out at the house today. Seems like I'm always thanking you."

He ate up the appreciation. "I don't mind at all. Pleasing you makes me feel good." The second the words were out, he wanted to call them back. No telling how she'd respond.

There was a pause, then, "Kenny," she said in a low, sultry voice. "I—" She cut herself off. "Vi just got here. I'll see you in the morning."

Surprising how the sexy way she said his name kicked up his attraction. Make that lust. He shook his head and returned to the table, where Buddha sat eyeing him. "What did Rose have to say?"

"Who says I was talking to her?"

"I saw the caller ID. I watched your face while you talked to her. That dopey smile you're wearing now... You like her."

Caught. Kenny groaned. "I'm doing my best not to get too into her. She's special, though."

"Remember, her husband just left her. She's nowhere near ready to start up with you, and you know it."

"She knows it, too."

"And how's that working out?" Kenny shrugged, and Buddha shook his head. "I'm not liking what I'm hearing and seeing, man. Haven't you suffered enough? You're headed for another boatload of misery. If it were me, I'd find a good therapist right away."

"I don't need one. She's handling the breakup really well and is busy and happy with the way her life's unfolding. Talented, too. I might hire her to help make my place look the way I want it to."

"What? That could cost a bundle."

"I won't ask her to do anything big, just give me ideas. She's amazingly creative."

Buddha eyed him. "You're sleeping with her."

"No." But he thought about it all the time. "I can't help the way I feel. But hey, don't worry. She doesn't want kids, and you know what I think of that."

"I still see trouble ahead. Maybe you should sign up with a couple of dating apps and get to know a woman who isn't going through a breakup or divorce."

"I've been thinking about that," Kenny said. The night of his mom's birthday party, he'd looked into a few sites. But he couldn't muster much enthusiasm for the idea and kept putting it off.

"Get on it. The sooner the better."

CHAPTER 16

Across town, Rose and Vi sat across from each other at Sweet Sue's. Unlike many restaurants, this one was relatively quiet despite the almost full dining room. Credit the plush carpeting and relatively high ceilings. Soft lights and crisp white tablecloths, each with their own tiny vase of hothouse flowers, added to the ambiance. Definitely a swishy place. No rushing through the meal, either. So far, they'd sipped cocktails and nibbled appetizers at a leisurely pace. The server, a handsome, dark-skinned man named Amir who looked to be in his late twenties or early thirties, was knowledgeable, friendly, and attentive.

"I haven't eaten here since senior prom," Rose said.

Vi smiled. "You're lucky your date could afford it."

"Oh, he couldn't. His parents paid the bill. You've been home almost a week now, and I haven't heard anything about your honeymoon. Tell me everything. Well, except for the juicy details."

Vi laughed. "It was wonderful. The weather was amazing!

The food, the hotel, swimming in the Caribbean Sea at least once a day and sometimes again in the early evening. We had an unforgettable time."

She radiated happiness Rose envied. Deep love and an adoring husband must be wonderful. Maybe someday she'd want that, too—if she fell in love. Right now, she wasn't the least bit interested in falling for anyone. Including Kenny. She was hot for the guy and liked him, but was nowhere near anything serious. "I'm dying to see photos."

"I have a zillion to show you, but I don't want to spend the entire evening looking at them. You can do that another time, but here are a few of our favorites."

Rose oohed and aahed, then Vi put her phone away. "Catch me up on you. First, I want to hear about the apartment you found. Congrats on that, by the way."

Rose gave her some of the details. "I can't wait for you to see it."

"I will, as soon as you're all moved in. Face-to-face conversation is so much more interesting than trading texts. I want more info. How are you really coping, how's school, are you enjoying the internship—and anything else I've missed."

Vi had a tendency to mother her, a holdover from their childhood, that at times was irritating. "Pepper me with questions, why don't you," Rose muttered. "Strike that. For the most part, life is good." She told her sister about school and how happy she was to be learning and interning at Thompson's. That working at Panache was so-so but a necessity she needed to get used to. "Your turn again. How's work? I'll bet it's hard to be back."

"Not really. There's only so much lazing around a person can do. Work is going real well."

The salads arrived, and they paused until Amir headed off to another table. Then Vi filled her in on the latest at DD Telecom, where she was an executive VP. She loved her job. If Rose was able to secure a position with Thompson after she graduated, she'd no doubt be every bit as happy. Under the table, she crossed her fingers that Tommie and Leigh would offer her full-time work there.

As they enjoyed the main course, Vi squinted at her. "Let's get down to the nitty-gritty, okay? Something about you is different. Your positive attitude, I think. That's amazing, considering all you've been through the past few weeks. Going back to school was a smart move."

"Thanks for noticing. I feel really good about school. I don't miss Peter at all, although I still want to strangle him."

"I'll happily support that. I can't imagine living in that house when it's all torn up."

"Like I said when you called from the Virgin Islands, he paid me upfront to stay and keep an eye on things. Did I mention he also wanted me to get rid of all the stuff he left behind? That's a lot of work." She lowered her voice. "Which is why I charged him a bunch to do it, and why I'm profiting in other ways. When I asked him what he expected me to do with all the furniture still in the house, he said it was up to me. I'm taking advantage of that." She explained about the antiques.

Vi gaped at her. "You've turned into a savvy business-woman. I'm so impressed."

Friends and Kenny had expressed the same admiration, but coming from her super smart, successful older sister meant the world. Rose grinned. "I learned from the best."

"I don't deserve credit for that."

"Sure you do. Growing up, I watched you and listened to you dealing with creditors and various bosses. I picked up quite a bit from you. And from Blake and Malcom. Both are brilliant."

"The fact that you listened and learned says a lot. Tell me about your apartment."

"It's tiny and so cute. Fully furnished, too. The bedroom has a big closet, which I'm going to love. You know how many clothes I have."

"Don't we all. Tell me, is Kenny doing a good job on the house?"

"Yes, and before I forget, he sends his congrats to you and Blake. He's super conscientious about his work." Rose told her about the leak in the bathroom and how from time to time he stayed later than the rest of his crew to complete a partly-done project. "He's been helpful to me, too. I ran into him at Pinole's last night—I treated myself after I signed the rental agreement. We ended up eating together, which turned out to be a good thing. My car battery was dead."

Although she didn't say another word about him, her sister slanted her head and slightly narrowed her eyes. "You like him."

How did she know? Rose sighed. "I do, but don't go getting ideas. I'm nowhere close to wanting another relationship. Kenny knows it, too. He has no interest in me, either. He wants a wife and kids. And you know how I feel about that." It was no secret Rose didn't want children.

"You two have discussed those things?"

"A little. Actually, a lot. Especially after the other night."

"You mean when your battery died?"

Rose shook her head. "Before that."

"Oh?" Vi said, all sing-song. Wide-eyed with curiosity, she leaned forward. "What happened?"

Me and my big mouth. Why had she said anything? Too late now. When Vi wanted info, she didn't stop till she got it. One of her shrewd business skills.

Amir appeared with dessert menus including the featured special that evening, which happened to be molten chocolate lava cake with house made ice cream. Both chocolate lovers, they each ordered a special. Meanwhile, Rose thought about how to answer Vi's question.

"You were about to tell me what happened," Vi reminded her when Amir left.

May as well talk about it. "Promise you won't judge me." When her sister signaled she wouldn't, Rose went on. "What happened is my fault." She filled Vi in on the corner of the mouth kiss that first time, when she'd aimed for his cheek. Then followed with the night of the kisses she couldn't get out of her mind. "I haven't had sex in a year, and Peter never was any good at it," she said. "That's no excuse for my behavior with Kenny. We'd been talking and looking at each other. I hugged him and he kissed me. He's such a good kisser." Remembering, she closed her eyes a moment and shifted in her seat.

"I know about kisses like that," Vi said with a dreamy expression of her own. "I had no idea until Blake kissed me. Go on."

"Then you understand how I felt. We kissed a few times, and it was pretty arousing. Before anything else happened, he pulled away. He doesn't want to be my rebound interest."

"I wouldn't want that, either."

"My feelings have nothing to do with a rebound. Like I

said, I'm not in love with Kenny, and he's not in love with me. At times, though, I think he's worried I might be. I'm sure some lucky woman will catch his eye." The thought temporarily ruined her appetite. "Face it, he's a gorgeous man. Also smart, kind, and encouraging about my career. He took the time to look at some of the designs I created on my iPad and was so enthusiastic.

"*And* he listens when I talk. Peter never did, zoned out instead. I just—" Amir was approaching with two mini cakes, and she finished in a low voice. "For the past week, I stayed away from the house while he was there, doing my best to get rid of my strong desire to jump his bones. It didn't work. I like being with him and keep thinking about sex. Now you know everything."

"Happy Birthday," the waiter said, and lit the candle on her molten chocolate lava cake.

She smiled. "Thanks." The cake smelled so good, her appetite returned. For a while, neither she nor Vi said much except to rave over the exceptional dessert.

As they waited for the bill, which was sure to cost a mint, Rose thanked her for a wonderful evening. Vi had yet to comment on her feelings about Kenny. Wanting her opinion and advice, she frowned. "You haven't said a word about what I told you."

"It's a lot to wrap my arms around. I get what you're saying about sex, especially when the chemistry between you is so strong. In my experience, nothing is ever about sex, period. It complicates matters, sometimes in ways you can't imagine. I know because I've been there. In the end, everything worked out for me, but I wasn't going through a divorce or a breakup. Blake wasn't, either, but we still had issues."

"Kenny says the same thing about the complications that could arise."

"Smart man. You're dealing with the end of your marriage and a life without Peter. As bad as things were between you and him, it's hard to see clearly." Vi thought a minute. "I don't want you to get hurt. Promise me you'll tread carefully."

"I will. I am."

Outside, Rose thanked her again for the evening. "Let's get together again soon."

"I'd love that. Blake and I will have you over for dinner."

"That sounds fun." They hugged each other, two sisters who were also close friends.

"We still need to schedule a dinner with Gran and Malcom," Rose said.

"Let's work on that soon." Once outside, they hugged each other goodbye. "Good luck with whatever you do," Vi said, "and remember, I'm always here for you."

AFTER A DAY of hard physical labor, Kenny usually fell asleep as soon as his head hit the pillow. Not last night. The seductive tone of Rose's voice when she'd called had set his body burning. He couldn't go on like this. He thought about Buddha's parting words to find someone else for distraction but knew he wouldn't. Right or wrong, Rose was the woman he wanted. She wanted him, too. Question was, what to do about it?

Unable to rest, he got out of bed and worked on the house until he was dead on his feet. That did the trick, and he finally dropped off. It was one way to deal with his hunger for her and finish the house sooner.

"Good morning," she said when he arrived. "Will the crew be here soon?"

"Another fifteen minutes or so. Did you and your sister have a good time?"

"The best. Have you eaten at Sweet Sue's?"

"No, but I've heard good things about it."

"It's a beautiful restaurant. Quiet, too, and the servers don't rush diners through the meal. Very romantic, but nice for anyone. The food is outrageous!" She described the meal, then paused. "There I go, yakking away. How was your evening?"

Like always, he didn't mind listening to her. "It was great. I beat Buddha in the first game and he beat me in the second one. Our dinner was mediocre, but that's how it is at a bowling alley. I have a question for you. I'm remodeling/refurbishing my house. I'll be finished soon. I'm lousy at decorating. Would you be interested in giving me advice? I'll show you around to give you a feel for the place. Just know it's not fancy like this house."

"I don't care about that. I'm flattered you want my opinion and agree I should see the place to take measurements and get ideas. Do you know what you like in terms of colors or anything else?"

He liked her. "I'm gonna need help there, too. Don't worry, I'll pay you for your time."

"I'd love to do that, but can I think about it and let you know when I get back this afternoon? I'm planning to visit consignment furniture stores with photos of the non-antique stuff I want to get rid of."

Why the hesitation? "When you asked me questions I assumed you were interested—"

"Believe me, I am. But—"

The sound of the crew tromping up the stairs put an end to the conversation way too soon. Shortly after they arrived, Rose left for class.

CHAPTER 17

During class, Rose thought about Kenny. It'd be fun to explore decorating ideas for his house. The thing was, although she had confidence in her ability and good taste and eventually wanted clients of her own, she wasn't sure she was ready now. She'd never visited someone's home and given advice. How did that work, anyway? The last thing she wanted was to waste Kenny's time and money on ideas unsuited to what he wanted. She didn't have a clue what his tastes were. From what he said, he didn't, either. How did a decorator go about finding out?

She considered asking Tommie for advice, but the woman had things to do and left shortly after the second class ended.

After days of stratus clouds, the weak winter sun was shining, making for a pretty day. Before going home, Rose changed her mind about visiting consignment furniture stores and decided to look at online reviews instead. Meanwhile, deep in thought about working with Kenny on his house, she strolled around campus, hardly noticing the cold air until her nose started running and her fingers grew stiff and numb despite her gloves. Time to get in the car and go home.

On the drive back, both excited and nervous about her first real decorating job, she gave herself a pep talk. Kenny didn't have ideas of his own, and it was up to her to get him thinking about what colors and styles he leaned toward. When she saw the house, she'd ask questions designed to help with that and use the answers to come up with ideas that worked for him. If he rejected them, she'd ask more questions and come up with new ones. "It'll be fun and will all work out," she assured herself out loud.

She was almost home when she realized the underlying issue that was giving her pause—her growing desire for him. "I'm a professional," she stated aloud, and pledged to focus on the business at hand, namely her suggestions and his opinions of them.

She arrived at the house shortly before noon. Kenny was there, but no one else seemed to be around. "What are you doing back so early?" he said. "I thought you were checking out consignment furniture shops."

"I decided to do that online instead. Where's the crew?"

"Taking their lunch break. Have you made up your mind about helping me out?"

"Yes, and I'm looking forward to it. Because you're my first client ever and I haven't completed my schooling, I'll give you a discounted fee. Give me your address and tell me when and what time."

She handed him her phone and he added the information. "We'll finish up here around five. How about after dinner? Unless you have plans."

"Nothing, really." Business was business, but there was no

reason why she couldn't seduce him once that part of the evening ended. Appalled at the idea she'd conjured up, she pushed it away. And was glad he wasn't a mind reader.

"Maybe if we have time after, you can drive me by your apartment," he said, then left to take his own lunch break.

Rose fixed herself what'd become her usual lunch since the demise of the kitchen—chips and a PB&J sandwich. She decided to check out some of the consignment shops after all. Several hours later, she returned home. The entire time she'd been out, she'd stewed about the evening ahead. It could either be a smashing success or a dismal failure.

Time would tell.

* * *

ROSE SHOWED up right on time, and just as Kenny finished tidying up his place. Between renovating Peter's house and his own, he hadn't had much time to clean. Freshly vacuumed, dirty dishes in the dishwasher, and the kitchen and bathroom cleaned, the place looked decent enough.

"Come in," he invited, wondering what she'd think of it. Compared to where she currently lived, it was no great shakes. She entered along with a gust of fresh, frigid air, her cheeks red from the cold. "Did you have trouble finding me?"

"Not at all. A ranch-style house." She glanced around, and he tried to see it through her eyes. Hardwood floors and rugs in the hallway and living room, the couch and chairs that'd seen better days. "Nice hardwood floors."

He liked that. "She's an oldie, built in the mid-fifties. I've updated the plumbing, wiring, insulation, and windows, but there's still a lot to do."

She'd already taken her coat off. He caught a whiff of the sweet scent he'd come to anticipate and hung it up in the closet. In a soft-looking pullover, a somewhat snug skirt that didn't fall quite to her knees, and low-heeled pumps, she was the picture of professional. Sexy professional. She had great legs.

Her eyebrows lifted a fraction, and he realized she'd noticed him checking her out. He cleared his throat. "Why don't I give you the grand tour?"

She nodded and pulled a notebook from the leather tote she took to class and her internships. "Would you mind if I take photos and measurements? They'll come in handy when I draw the sketches."

"Not at all." He looked forward to seeing what she put together.

"The house has a daylight basement with an extra bedroom and bath."

"Why don't we start there?"

She remained highly focused on the rooms and his replies to her questions. Why that turned him on even more was anyone's guess. On the main floor, she snapped lots of photos and made notes. She took a long look at the newly-finished master bedroom. Good thing he'd made the bed.

"Tell me about this," she said, gesturing around.

"When I bought the house, there were three bedrooms and a small den on this floor. One of the bedrooms was slightly bigger than the other two. I tore out the wall between the den and the largest bedroom to make this master." Was it his imagination or wishful thinking that she stared at the king-size bed? *Keep your mind on business.* "The other two bedrooms are for guests and kids when I have them."

"Got it."

They continued through the rest of the house. Between jotting down his answers to her questions, and other notes, measurements, and photos she snapped, getting through the entire house took the better part of an hour.

"Let's sit down and talk," she said when the tour ended. In the living room, they sat in the two mismatched armchairs facing a coffee table and couch. "There's a lot to do here. I think we should focus on this room and see how that goes." He nodded and she went on. "This is a decent-size. What do you envision here?"

"Something cozy and not all beat up. The coffee table's ancient, and the furniture is ratty-looking."

"I agree about the coffee table, but the furniture isn't too bad. If you get the cushions restuffed and recover the pieces with new fabric, you'll change the entire look of the room. I suggest a new area rug, too." They discussed colors using the color wheel she'd brought.

"I'll get the sketches done within the next few weeks," she said. "Why don't you come to Thompson's tomorrow and look at colors and carpeting, et cetera. You can take home samples and see how they look right here at home, where the light is different from the show room. I finish at four, so come before then."

"Great idea." He wanted her to stay longer and realized he hadn't offered her anything to eat or drink. "If you're hungry or thirsty, I have chips, pretzels, pop, wine, beer, or water."

"Nothing to eat, thanks, but pop sounds good."

"Got it. I'll be back shortly."

When he returned, she'd moved to the sofa. Her skirt rode slightly up her pretty legs. Talk about dangerous. Hardly aware of what he was doing, he sat down beside her, maybe a little too close. If so, she'd let him know.

"Walking and talking is thirsty work," she said after taking a sip. "This is just what I needed. You're my very first client. How did I do?"

"Really well. I'm impressed. You're going to have a stellar career."

Her smile dazzled him. "Thanks, but maybe hold off on the praise until you see the sketches."

How he wanted her.

He knew by her own longing looks that she wanted him, too. But they'd agreed not to go there, and he behaved himself. He mustered every ounce of willpower to keep his hands off her. Sitting near her was torture. Wanting her gone, he stood and drained his Dr. Pepper. "I don't know about you, but I'm bushed. I'll get your coat."

"This was fun. Thanks for asking me over. If I don't see you in the morning, I'll see you at Thompson's."

He walked her out the door. "Drive safe," he said, relieved she was leaving.

Inside again and too wound up to sleep, he prowled around the house, thinking about what he wanted the fixed-up version to look like. He paid special attention to the living room, where she wanted to start, but was too distracted to concentrate. Right now, his overpowering desire for her outweighed everything else, including remembering to drive by her apartment.

He doubted he could put off what he wanted much longer.

CHAPTER 18

On the drive home from Kenny's, Rose's mood vacillated from upbeat—the design part had gone well —to the disappointment that'd followed. Despite deliberately hiking her skirt inches above her knees and otherwise attempting to entice him into kissing her and more, she'd been rebuffed. The man wanted her, and she wanted him, so why not put them both out of their misery with a kiss or three and go from there? Rhetorical question when they both knew passions could quickly ignite into much more. Which was exactly what she wanted. Darned man was too worried about the possible fall out to lay a hand on her. Ah, well, maybe next time.

She went to bed in low spirits but slept surprisingly well. Thursday, she woke up with a plan to fix the problem. Not right away, but this afternoon. Business first at Thompson's. When that ended, she'd convince him that the last thing she wanted was a rebound relationship. Plain and simple, she had needs, and he was the man to satisfy them.

When Kenny texted a thirty-minute ETA, she replied that

she planned to get to Thompson's early and that she'd see him there that afternoon. Then she left.

Taking care of customers was enjoyable. She fielded questions without stumbling too much and guided more than a few people toward samples of wall colors, tiles, and flooring. She was a whiz at using the employees-only computer to access product information and availability and steering customers to consumer-friendly websites.

The hours passed quickly and she had to pinch herself for what she'd begun to think of as a dream internship leading to a dream job right there at Thompson's. This was where she wanted to be permanently, but she'd wait another week to ask about that, just to make sure.

As the clock ticked toward four o'clock and the end of her shift with no sign of Kenny, she began to doubt he'd make it. She was chatting with a middle-age man looking for ideas for his bathroom, when she sensed eyes on her. Turning her head, she saw Kenny. There went her stomach, all flip-floppy with excitement. "My appointment has just arrived," she told the customer. "Don't worry, Arlene at the counter will be happy to guide you."

"But I want to work with you."

"I'm an intern here and only work Tuesdays and Thursdays, but if you like, we can schedule an appointment for next Tuesday." She handed him a business card. "I don't have my own cards yet, but my contact information is on the back."

"Thanks," he said and pocketed it.

"If you want help now, Arlene has been here for a long time and knows a lot. I'm happy to introduce you."

Signaling Kenny that she'd be with him shortly, she introduced the customer to her fellow employee. Then, pulse hammering, she approached Kenny and tried not to drool. He'd taken off his jacket. In leather work boots, jeans that fit great, and a smoky blue, long-sleeve Henley T that emphasized his broad shoulders and chest, it was hard not to.

"Apologies for coming a little late," he said, shooting her that million-dollar smile. "Nice dress and tights."

She glanced down at her charcoal-color cashmere crew neck dress and patterned hose, which she'd bought at Panache the week before Peter had dropped his bomb.

On her best professional behavior, she offered a friendly smile in return. "Do you want me to show you around, or would you rather explore on your own?"

"I came here for you. I want your help."

Of all times for her nipples to perk up. She did her best to play nonchalant. After a quick tour of the store, she answered questions, then directed him to several books to look through. "I suggest you take a few books and samples home with you to look through. I told you about that last night."

"I remember. Will you come over and look at the samples with me?"

The invitation she'd been counting on. "Of course. I want to talk to you anyway."

"About decorating?"

"That, too."

"What else?" he asked, stroking his chin in thought.

Not about to get into a conversation about sex in public, especially at Thompson's, she lowered her voice. "It's a private matter."

His eyes smoldered. "Isn't it time for you to leave?"

She checked her watch, surprised at how the time had flown since he'd come in. "Past that. Why don't you fill in the forms for the books and samples you're borrowing while I say goodbye to Arlene. I'll drive to your house and meet you there."

"Works for me."

She headed over to Arlene. Leigh had already left for the day.

"Who's the hunky guy?" her peer asked. In her early fifties and happily married, she made no secret of the fact that she enjoyed looking at men of all ages. Who didn't?

"That's Kenny."

"The guy remodeling your ex's house. You never mentioned his looks." She pantomimed fanning herself.

Rose laughed. "He's also in the process of decorating his house, which he's just about finished renovating and remodeling. I'll be helping him figure out colors and designs tonight."

"That sounds interesting. Don't do anything I wouldn't have done at your age." She winked.

Rose headed toward Kenny, who stood waiting at the exit. "What did Arlene say?" he asked as they stepped into the dark cold.

"She thinks you're hot."

By the grimace on his face, he didn't care for that. "She looks like she's my mom's age, too old for me."

"She's happily married, just likes to look. See you at your house."

* * *

KENNY WHISTLED as he drove home. He'd decided to let his feelings out tonight, see what happened. It might not be the smartest move, but he wanted Rose and knew she felt the same way. Earlier that afternoon, on his way home from work to change clothes before visiting Thompson's, he'd stopped at a drugstore and bought a fresh box of condoms. He'd tossed most of them in the drawer of the table on his side of the bed. A couple went in his pocket. He'd changed the sheets, too. Couldn't hurt.

She didn't want kids, he reminded himself, and they didn't want a serious relationship with each other. This thing between them was about mutual satisfaction, period.

When she arrived at his house, he poured them each a glass of wine to sip while they sat a foot or so apart on the couch and looked through the samples and colors together. He wanted to move closer to her stayed put while they took care of the decorator stuff.

He told Rose what he liked and she nodded and jotted down notes. "I'll keep your choices in mind when I make those drawings. Give me a week to ten days?"

"No problem."

"Maybe you should pick up a few color samples of the paints that call to you and test them out in here and other rooms you're planning to paint. My recommendation is that you look at the colors both in daylight hours and at night."

"I will. It's about dinner time, and I'm getting hungry. You?"

"Yes, but I really want to talk before I go home."

Hoping the conversation had something to do with sex and nowhere near ready for her to leave, he brought up dinner. "I'm thinking we order teriyaki and eat here. Sound good?"

She agreed to that. While he ordered, she excused herself to use the bathroom.

"The food won't be here for a good thirty minutes, plenty of time to talk," he said when she returned. He patted a sofa cushion closer to him. She didn't object.

Her dress clung to her body just enough to hint at her curves. Sexy as hell. It wasn't easy to keep his hands to himself, waiting for her to say her piece. Trouble was, her scent knocked his brain for a loop. She smelled amazing, utterly irresistible. Setting the wine glasses on the coffee table, he sniffed appreciatively. "You smell really good tonight. What's the name of the stuff you're wearing?"

"You can smell that? I found a nice, lightly-scented bubble bath the other day, with body lotion to match. So you like it."

Like it? Images of her rubbing her lush body with lotion skyrocketed his desire. He wanted her like he'd never wanted a woman. "Listen, I've been doing some thinking."

"About this house. I know."

"That, but also about you and me."

"That's what I want to talk about," Rose said. "Please, let me go first." He gestured at her to speak. "I'm not looking for love, Kenny, so put the rebound business out of your head. What I want is a lover."

Exactly. He opened his mouth to agree, but she held up her hand, palm out, silencing him.

"Sitting with you last night, neither of us touching the other, was awful. I don't want to hide my feelings from you anymore, Kenny. I've known for days that I'm beyond ready for sex, and I think you want that, too."

He almost groaned with relief. "You have no idea how much. Before we go there, you should know that when I do settle down it will be with a woman who wants kids." He looked at her straight-on, letting her know he meant that.

"And I don't. We're good."

"I also need assurance that later you won't regret having sex with me," he added.

"I'll regret it if we don't."

She touched the tip of her tongue to the provocative dip in her upper lip, and he about lost his cool. Taking her at her word, he smiled. "Come here, you."

She scooted closer. "You've won the jackpot," she said in the same husky voice he'd heard on the phone when she'd called him from the restaurant the other night.

"Jackpot?" he asked, gazing into the mesmerizing pools of her eyes.

"You're about to get what you want. We both are." Her tempting lips parted a fraction. "Kiss me, or I swear, I'll die."

He tipped up her chin and captured her mouth.

CHAPTER 19

Rose lost herself in the pleasure of Kenny's lips on hers, his strong arms around her. Heaven. She forgot everything but here and now with him.

"God above, you taste good," he murmured without lifting his mouth from hers, as if he didn't want to pull back even for a moment. His passion set her yearning body on fire.

The kisses grew deeper and more fevered. Craving his hands on her, she unfastened the tiny string of buttons that ran halfway down the front of her dress, then arched her back. "Touch me."

His palms were already moving through the opening. He cupped her through the thin, lacy bra she'd selected just for him, teased his thumbs over her sensitive nipples. Moaning, she let her head fall back against the couch and simply enjoyed.

After a while he moved on, nuzzling her neck, sliding his palms up her calves. "Your legs are something else. I like the fancy diamond designs on those tights, too. You're so hot."

He had no idea. Already, she was wet with need. As he

smoothed his hands higher and reached her thighs, he made a sound of surprise. "These aren't tights."

She laughed, hardly recognizing her own throaty sound. "They're thigh highs. I'm happy to take them off."

"Are you kidding? They're sexy as hell. Leave them on but get rid of the panties."

All her lady parts rejoiced. Breathless, she obeyed. "What about you?"

"Forget about me."

Reaching up to the couch, he grabbed the afghan and laid it on the carpet, adding a throw pillow. "I want you right there on the floor, where I can look at you."

He knelt in front of her. Feeling self-conscious—men usually wanted to get her into bed and didn't spend much time studying her—and eager for what was coming, she lay back and closed her eyes.

He parted her thighs and looked at her most private part. "You're so beautiful."

Down there? "Stop looking and get busy, will—"

He let out a low laugh. "Impatient, are you? All right."

The next thing she knew, his tongue was right there on the pulsing nub that ached the most. He raised his head and grinned. "Is this what you want?"

"Yes," she said, and moaned, raising her hips and legs up.

He went back to business, also slipping fingers inside her. Within seconds, she climaxed, long and hard. When she finished, she was panting. "OMG, that was amazing."

He wore a satisfied expression. "You were ready."

"Didn't I tell you?" She'd never experienced such an intense orgasm, not with anyone. "So far, you're an excellent lover. She nodded at the arousal straining against his fly. "Your turn."

"I want our first time to be in my nice, big bed, where we can go wild and—" The sound of the doorbell interrupted. "That's our food."

While he answered the door, she stepped quickly into her panties and met him in the kitchen, where they washed their hands and set the table. "The food smells great," she said. "I'm hungry."

He grinned. "I'm not surprised."

They sat across the kitchen table, making small talk and enjoying the meal, which was delicious. Rose felt wonderful. "Can I tell you something no one else knows?" He set his fork down and nodded. She so appreciated the way he listened when she spoke. "I don't think I ever had a real orgasm until now."

His eyes widened and his eyebrows drew together in puzzlement. "What?"

"It's true. I didn't realize until you gave me so much pleasure. More than I ever guessed was possible." She smiled at him.

"That's quite a compliment."

"Well deserved." She put on a pouty face. "It's not fair, Kenny. I haven't given you any thrills."

"Trust me, I got a few. Making you crazy was a big turn on." His eyes went hot. "And that was a mere taste of what's ahead." He stood and reached across the table to grasp her hands and pull her up. "Ready go to the bedroom and explore each other?"

Desire made her knees weak. "I can hardly wait."

* * *

As badly as Kenny wanted Rose's first time with him to be in his bed, getting all the way up the stairs proved to be a challenge. Due to her. She stopped on the way up to unbutton his shirt and run her soft hands over his chest and all the way down to the waistband of his jeans. *Have mercy.* If that wasn't enough, she unzipped his fly with bold fingers. On the verge of losing control, he removed her hand, clasped it firmly in his, and rushed up the stairs.

In no time, they were both naked and checking each other out.

"You are one magnificent man," she said, her gaze traveling from his face down to his feet and back up to his hard-on.

Way to raise his hunger to the breaking point. "You're the beautiful one." His hands shook a little as he touched her sweet, bared breasts and nipples taut from the attention he gave them. "Lie down with me."

"Wait a minute," she said, breathless with lust. "I'm on the pill, but I think you should use a condom, too, just in case. I don't want to take any chances of getting pregnant."

He understood and had no interest in even thinking about that right now.

Once he pulled the covers back, he tumbled onto the bed with her. Long, deep kisses followed. As much as he enjoyed the foreplay, the urge to be inside her quickly drowned out everything else. He pulled away to sheathe himself, then in one thrust entered her. Seconds later, they climaxed together, one astounding orgasm that rocked his world. For several moments afterward, they lay silently entwined until sanity returned.

She let out a contented sigh. "That was unbelievable."

Mind-numbingly fantastic. He tucked her hair back behind her ears. "I wanted to make it last, but I couldn't hold back any longer."

"If you had, I'd have dropped dead of impatience."

He laughed. "I'd call it enthusiasm. You have that in spades." He gestured at the disheveled bed. "Look what our passion for each other did. The comforter is in a heap on the floor, the sheets are at the foot of the bed, and we're both too satisfied to care." He planted a tender kiss on her lips. "Let's do this again, once I recover."

"Fine with me." She smiled. "While we're waiting, do you want to drive by the house where my apartment is?"

"I think we should shower first."

"But you need time to recover."

"And I will, in the shower."

"That sounds intriguing. I confess, I've never showered with a man."

"Another first tonight?" Beyond pleased, he climbed over her to stand on her side of the bed. Offering her a hand up, he led her into the master bathroom.

Sometime later, dazed and sated, he handed her a bath towel and fastened another around his waist. "How did you like sex in the shower?"

"I feel like a limp straw, satisfied and sucked clean—and it's all your fault." She made a snorting sound. "I can see by your cocky smile how proud you are of yourself."

The words and her passion made him feel like a god. "I am." He planted a quick kiss on her lips. " I mean it now—I really need a break. It's still early. Let's get dressed and take that drive now."

CHAPTER 20

Excited to show Kenny her soon-to-be new home, Rose pointed ahead. "Pull over in front of that house." It wasn't far from his place.

He braked to a stop. Interior lights shone through closed drapes. "Looks like a nice place. Is the apartment upstairs or in the basement?"

She pointed to the dark window on the second floor. "Up there."

"Too bad the lights aren't on."

"Wish I could show it to you now. It's such a cute place. Once I get moved in, I'll invite you over to see it."

"Cool. We haven't had dessert. Wanna get some?"

She really did. "How did you know?" She glanced at the digital clock on his truck. "Well, shoot, Melissa Ann's closes at eight, and it's almost that now. We won't make it in time."

"Pinole's makes a good cannoli," Kenny said. "Hey, that rhymes."

"You're a poet." She'd never considered the sweets at the pizzeria. "You seriously want to get your dessert there?"

He nodded. "They have several flavors. One of my favorites has chocolate chips in the filling. The cinnamon and pistachio is also good."

She was already licking her lips. "I'm in." What a great end to a fun night.

He grinned. "Let's get one of each to go and eat at my place."

And maybe have sex again? She didn't ask, but she wanted it. Instead of sating her sexual appetite, making love with Kenny had increased it exponentially. Better not be falling for him. *I'm not,* she assured herself. Sex and friendship was all she wanted.

Back at his house, they dug in. Delicious. Soon, they were feeding each other bites. So romantic and sexy.

"I'm getting turned on," he said. "Want to go to bed?"

"Yes, please."

* * *

KENNY LOVED everything about sex with Rose. Her body, the taste of her, her passion and willingness to try new things. She was the most passionate woman he'd ever been with. More in control than he'd been earlier, he took his time, pleasuring her and thoroughly enjoying what she did to him in return. He didn't think he'd ever get enough of her.

When they finished, he snuggled her closer. "I like having you in my bed. I could get used to this."

Get used to it? Right away, he knew he shouldn't have phrased his feelings that way. He didn't want her getting the wrong idea. Damn his big mouth for spewing out the words without a conscious thought.

She gave him a long, questioning look, and he knew he'd sounded way too into her and too serious, when he wasn't even close. *Oh, yeah?* a small voice in his head taunted. He wasn't, he assured himself. Heck, no.

Eager to repair any damage his words might have caused, he hurried to explain. "I don't know why I said that. My mouth got ahead of my brain. I like you, Rose, and I sure enjoy the sex. Our friendship, too. What I said is based on lust. I haven't had a woman in my bed for a while now, and having you being here with me is..." He paused and searched for what to say that wouldn't make her tense up again. "Well, it's hot. You're as into it as I am."

"You're right about that," she said, but pulled away, scooting closer to the edge of the bed. Emotionally, too, he sensed.

He was no great shakes at reading women but figured his explanation had somehow been off. "Everything okay?" he asked and caught his breath.

"Of course." She flashed a quick smile that fell shy of its usual dazzle, as if much was left unsaid. "I'm totally sated and really tired." She reached for the rumpled sheet and covered herself. Modesty now, when he'd tasted and touched her entire body? "Panache is having a sale next weekend, but there are bound to be customers looking for bargains early. I need a good night's sleep."

Still holding the sheet, she sat up and swung her legs over the bed.

It made sense that she wanted to get her rest. So that was the problem. Relief washed through him, and he could breathe again.

She gathered her clothes from the floor and padded into

the bathroom. Soon after, she emerged fully dressed. He sat up.

"Stay where you are, Kenny. I'll let myself out. Goodnight."

No goodbye kiss? She didn't quite meet his eyes, either. That and her slightly cooler tone of voice told him she wasn't okay, after all.

What if she'd expected him to say something more romantic? He sure hoped she wasn't falling for him.

CHAPTER 21

At home, relieved to have the following day and upcoming weekend away from Kenny, Rose lay in bed and thought about the magical hours they'd shared.

Making love with him had been more than she'd ever imagined it could be, the sexual highlight of her life. She didn't regret one second of it. Her body was still purring with satisfaction. She'd bet money the next time would be just as mind-blowing. Too bad she'd never find out, no matter how much she wanted to.

What he'd said—that he could get used to her lying in his bed—and the way he'd treated her like she was special in a way no man ever had was exceptional, yet made her nervous. Already, he cared too much. She worried he was falling in love with her.

And here he'd been worried about *her* falling for *him* as a rebound thing. She was fine with a physical-only... What was a good word for what they shared? Friendship, she'd call it. He'd used the same word. Forget love. Credit Peter for ruining the whole idea of that. Yes, her feelings for Kenny kept growing, but that was due to the great sex, she assured herself.

It seemed that for him, the opposite had happened. Oh, the irony.

The following morning, knowing he and his crew would arrive around eight, she made herself a sandwich for lunch, then ate breakfast, showered, and dressed for work, finishing minutes before he texted his ETA. She also stewed over what to say to him and how to act. Normally, she decided, friendly like always. She saw no reason to talk about the previous night, not with the crew sure to arrive shortly after him.

"Hi," she said, feeling slightly ill-at-ease when he let himself in.

"Morning. How did you sleep?"

He glanced at her lips. As always, heat flooded her. There'd be no more of that. Ignoring her strong attraction, she busied herself filling the to-go cup with coffee. "Really well, thanks. Today and the weekend will be exhausting, but if I have time I'll work on those drawings for your house."

"That'd be great, but no rush." He looked her over. "When you left last night, things felt strained between us. They still do. I hope that doesn't last."

"Me, too." Unless he was falling for her. Then everything would change.

He opened his mouth, then shut it. "We should talk."

Not now. She wasn't ready. "Can it wait? I'll be leaving soon. Tell me what you'll be doing here today."

"We've been making good progress on the kitchen, but today we'll set that aside and start on the master bedroom."

"I'll get my things out of there, then." It was a good thing she'd been slowly moving her things into the guest bedroom. "After that, the master bath?"

"That's right. Then we'll finish the kitchen."

Small talk was easier than anything serious. "Peter will be glad things are moving along so well."

As the crew tromped toward the door, she pulled her coat from the closet. She slipped into it and greeted them. "I'm off to Panache. Happy Friday to you all and have a good weekend."

* * *

To Rose's surprise, Friday zipped by. That evening, needing to talk about Kenny, she tried to reach Ragan and Pressley. Neither was home. She left messages and phoned Vi.

"I was just about to call you," her sister said. "TGIF. As much as I love my job, the past few days have been hectic. We can talk about that later. I know this is a spur-of-the-moment invite and we saw each other Tuesday night, but if you haven't had dinner would you want to meet at Come on In? Blake's gone out with friends and I'm not in the mood to eat alone."

Rose brightened right up. "I'd love to. I just got home from Panache and really don't want to microwave anything. Plus, I need to talk to you." She wanted her sister's take on Kenny and what had happened. "I can get there in twenty minutes."

"Talk, huh? Now I'm super curious. I'll leave shortly and get us a table. See you soon."

The parking lot at the diner was full as it tended to be Friday nights, but Rose managed to find a spot. She headed inside, where the noise level was loud but not deafening. All the tables were full, and she spent a minute searching for Vi. Her sister had snagged a table for two. Perfect.

"How did you get such a great place to sit?" Rose said when she reached her sister.

"As I walked in, I saw a couple about to leave. So I claimed it. Need a menu?"

Rose shook her head. "I already know what I want."

Vi signaled for a server, and an older woman bustled over. When she left with their orders, Rose settled in to talk. Before she shared about Kenny, she wanted to hear about Vi. "How was work today, and why were the past few days so hectic?"

Her sister rubbed her temples. "Seemed like everyone needed help with something. I'm glad for the weekend."

"I don't blame you. Who's Blake out with tonight?"

"One of his closest friends, Ross. Working together, you'd think they'd get tired of seeing each other."

Rose detected irritation there. "You're mad at him."

"More disappointed. We've both been so busy this week, and I was looking forward to an evening alone together. I guess the honeymoon spoiled me. But we'll have tomorrow and Sunday. Enough about me. What's new with you? How was your week? Start with Panache."

"There were a lot of customers in the store, hoping to find stuff today that goes on sale next weekend. A week too early, and they end up paying full-price. Sometimes that happens, and I sure don't mind." She shrugged. "I can't blame them and might do it myself if I didn't work there. Even with more customers than the usual, it wasn't nearly as hard as last Friday. I guess I'm getting used to working there. I don't love it, but I do like my paycheck. Can I run something by you?"

"Ah, what you want to talk about. Let me guess—it has to do with Kenny."

"You're right. A lot has happened since we had dinner together the other night. Which I'm still salivating over, by the way." Rose lowered her voice. "Let me backtrack to Wednesday, the first time he invited me over to see his place. He's been renovating and remodeling and wants me to help him figure out furniture placement and color schemes. We focused on the living room and left the rest for another time. I really enjoyed doing that. I'm proud that I'm finally going to get my degree. Anyway, my mind was strictly on business, taking notes and measuring things, but deep down, I wanted him. I could tell he felt the same way. I mentioned the conversation he and I had about that at Sweet Sue's."

Vi nodded. "The rebound thing."

"Anyway, the no-touch rule was hard to stick to, but we both behaved. So yesterday, he came to Thompson's to look at colors for fabric and walls. I helped him choose samples to take home. He invited me back to the house to give my opinion of how the samples looked there."

"Your first real client. What part of town is he in and what's his home like?"

"He's in the south end, and the house is nice. It's a 1950's style ranch that was a fixer-upper when he bought it but it looks pretty good now. He's almost finished—he works on it nights and weekends."

"There's a man who loves what he does for a living. He's a true talent."

"In so many different ways." Rose glanced down at her hands.

"That's one big sigh. I'm sensing the no-touch rule went

bye-bye." Vi leaned in and raised her eyebrows. "Talk, and don't leave anything out."

"By the time we finished discussing the living room, I was determined to seduce him. As it turned out, we seduced each other."

"I'm not surprised. And?"

"It was excellent." Rose exhaled loudly.

"I sense a 'but.' Let me guess—you're falling for him." Vi looked concerned.

"Not at all. I like the sex, but I'm not even close to loving him," she assured her sister and herself. She liked him an awful lot, period. "I'm worried he's falling for me."

"The opposite of what he was worried about. What makes you think so?"

Rose struggled to put her reasons into words. "The way he looks at me and listens carefully when I talk, like I really matter to him." Not that concerns about the possibility had gotten in the way of what she and Kenny had shared. "Not to get too detailed, but he seems more interested in my pleasure than his own." The mere mention of it made her want him.

"Sounds pretty good to me."

"Yes, but—" Rose caught herself chewing on her pinky fingernail and put her hand in her lap. "I'm still raw from the divorce and can't handle anything serious. Besides, he's mentioned wanting kids several times, and you know how I feel about that. Oh, here comes our food."

"You may not want kids, but you're going to be a fantastic auntie," Vi said while they ate. "What are you going to do now?"

"I don't know. I'm hoping you have suggestions."

Vi thought a minute. "I think you need to sit down together and iron things out."

"I would, but the thing is, I'm not sure of his feelings. If I misread him, I'll look like a fool saying I'm worried he cares too much."

"From my own mistakes and experience, I know talking is never a bad thing. Hashing out our problems has guided Blake and me through lots of misunderstandings. I guarantee you won't look like a fool, and you'll find out the truth. Speaking of feelings, are you sure of your own?"

Had her sister read something on her face when she didn't, *did not*, love Kenny? "Why are you asking when I said I'm not in love with him?"

"Just checking."

"I love you dearly, Vi, and I asked for your advice, but I'm not a little girl anymore. I don't need you to mother me, okay? I like being friends with Kenny and sharing little things with each other. As much as I enjoy the sex, I don't think it should happen again until I know where he's coming from."

"Then start the conversation there."

After dinner, Rose went home and worked on a scale representation of Kenny's living room. She also thought about Vi's advice. Maybe she should talk to him. Or not. There was no rush. She decided not to worry about it right now.

A week later when Saturday dawned, she woke up refreshed and ready for the brutally busy day ahead. She didn't think about Kenny at all. Well, not much. Gearing up for the day ahead was foremost. Although winter was in full force and would be for another month or two, Panache's weekend winter sale kicked off today. The company always hosted it at the beginning of February to pare down the winter inventory and make room for new spring fashions.

After a bigger breakfast than usual to boost her energy, she arrived at the store eager to work hard and sell a bunch of clothes and other items. Which, thanks to the commissions employees were paid, would net her a fat check. Melanie and Electra, the assistant manager, were there, too, along with Penny, another part-timer, to handle the customers. There were a lot of them coming and going, and Rose and the rest of the staff could barely keep up.

As busy as it was, working with customers who loved clothes as much as she did made for a fun and satisfying day. During a slow period midafternoon, a woman entered the store. She was pretty, and Rose guessed her to be in her mid- to late-forties.

"Hi," she greeted the customer, using her most welcoming smile. "How can I help you?"

"I've been waiting to come in until the sale. There are so many pretty things in here! My birthday was earlier this month, and my thoughtful older son gave me money to buy myself something pretty. I added it to my credit card, and here I am."

She was amiable and open, easy to like. "Let's find you a new outfit. What are you looking for?"

The woman studied her. "Something cute, like your dress and those tights."

Rose had donned a dark mint wool A-line dress and a pair of loden-green tights with tiny rhinestones up the back.

"I'm glad you like it. I don't know about this color palette for you, though."

"I'm thinking the same thing."

Rose studied her with a critical eye. "You'd look best in softer tones—peach, coral, amber."

While she'd been talking, the woman reached into her purse. "If you can, I'd like something to go with this scarf." She held up a sky-blue silk scarf with silver edging.

"That blue is gorgeous on you. By the way, I'm Rose."

"Brandy. Thanks. It was a birthday gift from my boyfriend."

"He has excellent taste."

"I knew that on the day he asked me out." Brandy laughed.

Admiring her confidence, Rose smiled. "I can think of several dresses to show you, but there are lots of other choices, too. Let's look around and find something you can't live without."

It didn't take long before Brandy found the perfect dress. "It looks like it was made for you," Rose said as the woman studied her reflection. "I know just the shimmery tights to go with it."

"Show them to me! I have to agree with you—I look good. I'm going to wear this outfit and the scarf tonight." Brandy sounded excited. "My sweetie's treating me to dinner and a comedy show at the Highway Club. He's the events planner there."

"How cool. He'll love that dress on you."

Brandy handed over her credit card. The last name was Martin. *Brandy Martin.* Rose was sure she'd heard the name before, but couldn't place it. "Your name sounds so familiar," she said.

"Does it? Maybe we've met somewhere. With only twelve-thousand people in Port Simms, we might have." She squinted slightly at Rose. "You look too young to have dated Kenny in high school."

"Kenny Martin is your son?" Rose was surprised and knew she looked it.

"You know him?"

Much better than she'd ever admit. "He's renovating my soon-to-be ex's house." She handed Brandy's credit card back.

The woman gave a slow nod. "Dr. Shafer. Kenny told me about him and that you're staying there while he fixes it up."

He'd told his mother about that? Rose didn't know what to think or say. "That's right," she said after a moment. He really knows what he's doing."

Brandy straightened up tall, all proud. "He's a very talented man."

He certainly was. Rose's cheeks felt hot. She hoped they weren't too red for Brandy to notice. "Thanks for coming in, Brandy. I enjoyed working with you."

"So did I. Wait'll I tell Kenny I met you."

Rose could only imagine that conversation.

KENNY WAS SIPPING coffee and testing paint colors on the walls late Sunday morning when his mom called. Grinning, he answered. "Hey, Mom, Happy Ground Hog Day. How are you?"

"Happy Ground Hog Day to you, too, she said and laughed. "I'm really good. Last night, Racer and I had dinner at the Highway Club and saw a comedy show. We had such a good time. He really liked the dress I bought yesterday— thanks to the birthday money from you. That was so sweet."

"You deserve. Send me a photo."

"I will. You'll never guess where I bought it. Panache."

Wasn't that where Rose worked? "Okay," he said, wary.

"Rose Shafer helped me find it. I like her, Kenny. Why haven't you told me you're dating her?"

He almost spewed his coffee and wondered what Rose had told her. "I'm not. Whatever gave you that idea?"

"Call it a feeling. She's gorgeous, Kenny, and really nice. I can't believe her husband left her. I shouldn't say this, but I'm glad he did. If he hadn't, you and she might never have met."

"We're not dating, Mom, so put that idea out of your head." But he loved the sex. Really liked her, too.

She started humming like she did when she sensed he wasn't being straight with her. They were having sex, not dating. Stifling a frustrated groan, he said he was working on the house and had to get back to it. They disconnected, and he shook his head.

Surely Rose hadn't said anything like that to his mother, a virtual stranger to her. Although, if she was in love with him, she might've.

He intended to find out.

CHAPTER 23

Sunday being the last day of the sale was another very busy time, and Rose stayed at Panache later than she was scheduled. With the sales she logged and the commission earned, she didn't mind. But she was worn out. The last thing she wanted was to go back to the unfinished mess at Peter's house. It didn't help that the furniture consignment people had cleared the living room and master bedrooms of the furniture they wanted, leaving only the guest bedroom set upstairs, the dining room set and chairs, and the desk, table and chairs in the den.

Staying at the house had become all but intolerable. February fifteenth, moving day, couldn't come soon enough. Melanie had given her the okay to take that day off, which was nice.

Having eaten hours ago, she needed food, but the thought of making due with the meager choices at the house wouldn't do. On the way home, she stopped and picked up fast food. With the house almost empty, where to sit and eat? The only possibilities other than the dirty floor were the sole chair in the dining room that wasn't piled with stuff or the table in the den.

The dining room was closer. After kicking off her shoes and getting rid of her tights, she plunked down and sighed. Already, her toes felt better. She glanced down at them and frowned. They were worse than her fingernails before she'd taken care of them. Of course, they weren't in a class with a spa mani, but until she started making decent money, the only option was do-it-yourself. She ought to do the pedi tonight but was way too tired. Besides, it was winter and not barefoot season, so no hurry. But going barefoot in winter wasn't fun. She dragged herself up the stairs to get her slippers, then trudged downstairs again.

After finishing the meal, she felt much better, could even think again. Her thoughts turned to meeting Kenny's mother and what she might've told him. There wasn't much to say except that they knew each other through the house. If she'd even said anything. Rose hadn't heard from him. He must be avoiding her like she was him. Although he'd been happy enough when she'd last seen him, a man fully sated.

Steering clear couldn't last forever, not with him in the house Mondays through Fridays. If only she knew how to find out his true feelings without asking, which she didn't want to do. She yawned so hard, her eyes watered. Tired as she was, it was way too early for bed. May as well make herself useful with drawings for his house, work that was always stimulating and sure to wake her up. With any luck, she might also hatch an idea or two about how to approach the subject of his feelings without making an idiot of herself.

Seated at a chair in the den, she reached across the table for her iPad and notes from the other night. After calling up the drawing app, she caught herself staring into space. As drained as she was, thinking and being creative were impossible. She was on the verge of dozing off when someone knocked at the door. No telling who that might be. With a heavy sigh, she pushed to her feet and padded toward the front door.

Kenny. Now, when she was an exhausted mess and had no idea how to go about coaxing him to admit his true feelings without embarrassing herself.

"I need to come in," he said, and she realized she'd been standing there in the cold, gaping at him.

"If you must." She let him in. "I'm asleep on my feet, too tired to work on those drawings. Believe me, I tried."

"I'm not surprised. Last weekend wore you out, too. It happens when you're burning the candle at both ends. Don't stress about the drawings. Like I said, take your time."

He hung up his coat. She wished he wouldn't. "What do you want?"

"Let's sit down and talk."

How she dreaded the sound of that. "Can't you tell me here?"

"Not with you about to keel over."

"All right. The only place to sit is in the den."

He followed her there and sat in one of the chairs at the table.

By the somber look on his face, he wasn't happy. That made two of them. She folded her hands on the table top. "Let me guess—this is about me meeting your mom at Panache. I didn't know who she was when I helped her find an outfit. She was fun to work with. All I knew was her first name until I saw the last name on her credit card. I mentioned I knew you, she asked how we met, and I told her. I didn't say anything else."

He made a swipe-the-forehead gesture. "That's a big relief. The way she talked made me wonder what you said."

"You think I'd tell her anything about us?" Rose snorted. "She's your mother. I helped her and I liked her, but I hardly know the woman. Even if I did, I wouldn't say anything. What happens between you and me is none of her business."

"Amen to that."

He seemed okay, except for his fingers tap-tapping the tabletop. In no mood to question him about his feelings or talk about the other night, she gave him a sideways look. "I'm failing fast. Is there something else you want to say before you leave and I fall into bed?"

He sat back, crossed his arms, and studied her through slightly narrowed eyes. "Are you in love with me?"

The unexpected question shocked her. "Absolutely not." Emboldened now, she mimicked his body language. "The real question is, have you fallen for me?"

* * *

How could Rose think he loved her? Kenny gaped at her. "Hell, no. I admire your talent, and I really like the sex. But love? No way. You know that, so why ask? Unless you have some ulterior motive."

She eyed him warily. "What motive could I possibly have?"

"I was only asking, okay?" He scratched his head, thinking. "This has to do with the comment that I could get used to you in my bed, am I right? The words spilled out, okay? The sex was so good, and my brain was mush. I explained that as soon as I said them. Guess you didn't believe me."

"No, I didn't."

"It's the truth."

After a minute, she nodded, but her arms were still crossed, as if she wanted to shield herself. "How could you possibly think I feel that way, when I've repeated multiple times that I have no interest in love? I'm nowhere near feeling anything like that for you."

"I'll tell you why. After I explained the thing I said, you pulled away from me. I thought because you were in love with me and understood I didn't love you back. FYI, I'm happy with our no-strings relationship."

The unhappy expression on Rose's face faded and she uncrossed her arms. "So am I. I guess we got the wrong idea about each other." Lips quirking, she shook her head. Then started to laugh, which made about as much sense as an iPad dancing.

"What's so funny?" he asked.

"We've both been worried about each other's feelings, and I..." Another hoot of laughter burst from her. "I don't know why I think that's funny. Must be fatigue," she said and laughed until her eyes watered.

He didn't see the humor in the situation but the laughter was contagious. Before long, he joined her.

After a while, the hilarity faded. "That felt so good," she said. "I've been a mess since I left the other night."

He felt better, too. "I guess we both needed to get rid of the tension. Humor was a great way to do it. Are we good now?"

"Yes, but I don't know what comes next."

"That depends. Do you want to keep having sex?" he asked.

"You have no idea how much. I'm guessing you do, too."

"It's on my mind all the time." Beast that he was, even now, when she was exhausted.

"Then we're agreed." She blew out a breath that sounded like relief.

"Not quite. We need to clarify something. You already know I'm looking to settle down with someone and start a family. Will it bother you if I date other women?"

"Not at all, and by the way, you and I aren't dating."

"You know what I meant."

"This is about clarity, and I'm making sure we're both clear about what's ahead. You deserve to find what you're looking for."

Problem solved. He grinned. "Then it's settled. We'll continue to be friends with benefits."

"Excellent."

"This calls for a hug." He stood and pulled her up close.

"Mmm," she said. "Our hugs always feel so good."

"Yeah." He wanted more than hugs and sensed she did, too, fatigue and all. "How about we seal the deal with those benefits we agreed on? If you're not too tired."

"For sex with you? No way—if you don't mind the boxes all over the guest room and me falling asleep after. In fact, I can't think of a better way to drop into la-la land. Do you have a condom with you?"

He nodded. "Boxes don't bother me, and I don't have any problem with you falling asleep. I'll even tuck you in and lock the door when I leave."

"I'm so glad we understand each other," she said, her brilliant smile ending in a yawn. "I guess I'd better brush my teeth first." She led the way upstairs.

Despite the fatigue, she rallied after warm-up foreplay. The sex was as great as it was before. "Good night," she murmured when it was over. Then with a satisfied sigh, she snuggled into the bed.

"Sleep well." He kissed her forehead, tucked the comforter around her, and left with a smile and happy body.

He really could get used to loving her on a nightly basis. Not loving *her*, which would cause him no end of suffering. Her body.

He almost believed it.

CHAPTER 24

The following week, Rose met Pressley and Ragan at Come on In for cocktails and appetizers. The diner had recently added a Happy Hour, which suited them all. "It feels like years since we talked," she commented when they gathered in a booth. "What's up with you two?"

"Marcus and I are planning a trip to Cabo in April," Ragan said. "The weather then should be perfect." She filled them in on the details.

Rose envied her. "That sounds fun." Of the few things she missed about Peter, the trips he'd paid for ranked high on the list. Plain and simple, she missed his money and what it could buy. Never mind, she was happy making her way without him.

"My breaking news is that I broke up with Jonathan," Pressley announced.

Rose had wondered. "You said you were thinking about it, but I never heard what happened. Did you, Ragan?" Her other friend shook her head. "It would've been nice to clue us in. Must've been fairly painless."

"Sorry I didn't let you two know. You knew it was going to happen. Anyway, we parted without a hitch." Pressley shrugged. "I guess he was getting tired of me, too. I'm ready to date again." She glanced at Rose. "You look different than you did last time I saw you. Terrific, in fact."

"I do?" Rose touched her hair. "I really need a cut and color, but right now I don't want to spend the money."

"I'm not talking about your hair, which looks fine to me. What's your secret?"

"So many things," Rose said and decided to save the news about Kenny for last. "I'm excited about my new apartment. My internship is the best. I love working there. I've been putting off asking Leigh and Tommie if I can stay on, but I will this Thursday."

"Cool!" Pressley said, and Ragan gave a thumbs-up. "I'll bet they'll welcome you."

"Give us details about the apartment," Ragan said. "When do you move?"

"In eleven days, but who's counting? It's the cutest! Fully furnished, with a nice, big closet. The landlords are great, and Melanie at Panache gave me the day off to move. Give me a few weeks to get settled and finish my final paper about the internship. It's due the last day of February, a few days before the end of the quarter. Then I'll have a party. You're invited."

"We'd better be," Ragan said in a fake stern voice. "That's a lot on your plate."

"It's not that bad. I've been staying after class on Mondays and Wednesdays to work on the paper. My goal is to finish the rough draft before the move. If that doesn't happen, my priority will be to get it done."

"It's hard to imagine you living solo," Pressley said. "You've been so insistent about living with other people."

"Partly because I was worried about having the money to pay the rent. You make the idea sound pretty good, and I want to try it. With what I made on selling Peter's unwanted stuff and the paychecks from the internship and Panache, I can actually afford the rent on my own, which feels amazing. I wish I could move tomorrow. Peter's house is such a mess."

"I meant to ask about that," Ragan said. "Renovations are rarely clean and easy, especially when the contractor juggles several jobs at the same time."

"Kenny doesn't do that, not with this house. He's getting paid too much to split his time with other jobs. Plus, he gets a bonus if he finishes on schedule."

Her friend narrow-eyed her. "As soon as you mentioned his name, you lit up."

Pressley nodded. "I noticed that, too. And you thought I should've told you about my break up. When were you planning to tell us that you and he are doing more than talking?"

"Why do you think I wanted to get together tonight? I've been saving the best for last." Rose flipped her hair and gave her friends a sultry look. "We're now officially FWB."

"FWB…" Pressley puzzled, then nodded. "Friends with benefits. So that's why you're glowing!"

"Every inch of me."

"It's about time you had good sex. When did that start?"

"About a week and a half ago."

"And all this time, I've been concerned about you," Ragan said. "You and Kenny are already getting serious? It hasn't been that long since Peter left."

Pressley scoffed at the woman. "She hasn't been in love with him in forever or had sex, remember? Have you forgotten when you were single and dating around? Not everything is about love. Sex is sex, and we all need it. Am I right, Rose?"

"Totally. Wanna know the best part about this? From the start, we've been upfront about what we want from each other. Like you said, Ragan, the last thing I want is to get into a serious relationship. Kenny's the opposite. He's ready to meet someone, get married, and have kids. We're aware our relationship won't last forever, and we're both okay with that."

Pressley frowned. "I'm confused. He wants to meet a woman and get married. How does that fit into your arrangement?"

Equally confused, Rose frowned. "I don't understand."

Her besties exchanged glances. This time, Ragan spoke. "I assume Kenny will be dating a lot to find that special person, but he isn't dating yet. Did I get that right?" Rose nodded, and she went on. "It seems to me that as soon as he starts going out with other women, the thing between you and him ends."

"It doesn't have to," Rose argued. "Who says he's going to meet The One that fast?"

"If he's intent on finding the future mother of his children, and meets a potential Mrs. Martin…"

Rose couldn't bear to think of him actually falling for someone, even if she had no right to feel that way. She chewed on her pinky.

"And there we have your answer," Pressley said. "To coin a cliché, you're playing with fire. And when you play with fire—"

"You get burned," both friends chimed in unison.

At the moment, he wasn't dating, and who knew when he would? For now, there was nothing to worry about. Rose shoved the unpleasant thought from her mind. Yet the warning stayed with her.

* * *

THURSDAY MORNING, Rose made sure to stay at the house till Kenny showed up. She'd been stewing about her besties' comments since the other night. Why hadn't she thought things through more carefully before deciding to be his friend with benefits?

Because she hungered for him so much now, she didn't think about the future. And because, want to or not and despite assuring herself otherwise, she was falling for him. Correction—had fallen. She hadn't told a soul and wasn't going to. What was the point? Because he wanted kids and she didn't, they could never be together.

He could start dating anytime. For all she knew, he already had. But wouldn't he have told her? Not so far, although the subject hadn't come up. She hadn't been with him since Monday and wanted to make sure she was foremost in his thoughts. A few ideas came to mind, namely, a tactic she'd tried with Peter with iffy results.

She could easily fail again. But Peter was gay, whereas Kenny was one-hundred percent hetero. Darn her for her insecurities. If only she were more sure of herself. Not much she could do about that, but giving him a few memorable kisses to keep his focus on her couldn't hurt.

When he let himself in, she was waiting. "Hi there," she said in her best flirty tone.

He gave her a sideways look. "What's up?"

"For starters, my internship will be ending next month. I'm going to talk to Leigh today about staying on at Thompson's. Wish me luck."

"Good luck, but you don't need it. If they don't take you, they're crazy."

"I certainly think so." She lowered her eyelids a fraction. "It's been three long days since we've been alone," she said and ran her fingers slowly up his chest." He groaned the way he did when he was turned on, and she smiled to herself. "But I have good news. Last night, I finished your drawings for the living room, and bonus, another for the master bedroom, scaled for each. Apologies it took me so long to get them done."

"To repeat myself, there was no rush. Plus, I only expected to see the one for the living room. I get the master bedroom, too? Cool. When do I get to see them?"

"There's not enough time now. How about after I finish at Thompson's this afternoon? I'll come over."

"With good news from Leigh," he said.

"You're always rooting for me, and it always turns me on." She touched her tongue to the dip in her upper lip to let him know she wanted to do more tonight than review the drawings.

His eyes burned with desire. "Any more of that, and we'll get in trouble this morning. I'll leave here early and meet you at my place no later than five o'clock."

Things were still good between them, and she flashed him a smile. "See you then. I have to go. As you can tell by the smell, the coffee's percolating." Moments before she put on her coat, wanting to leave him with extra heat, she beckoned him closer. "I forgot something."

"Me, too. There's something I should tell you—"

"Shh," she said, and cut him off. "Tell me tonight. This is more important." She pulled him down and kissed him with passion. "Have a great day."

When she left, they were both breathing hard.

CHAPTER 25

Kenny arrived home from work in time to shower and change clothes. He had something to tell Rose, had wanted to that morning, but she'd distracted him with flirty touches and a red-hot kiss. Maybe waiting until they had more time to talk about it was a better idea. Tonight then, preferably before they had sex. He doubted what he had to say would change anything, but his gut nudged him to talk before things got hot and heavy.

After she arrived and hung up her coat, he planted a welcome kiss on her lips.

"Hi." She pulled back and sniffed the air. "Do I smell fried chicken?"

"Delivered a few minutes ago. Hungry?"

She nodded.

"I'm keeping it warm in the oven. Did you talk to Leigh?"

Her beaming expression gave him the answer. "You're looking at the newest full-time employee at Thompson's. Or I will be when my internship ends."

He pulled her into a hug. "I'm so proud of you."

"I'm super stoked."

Her stomach rumbled loudly and he chuckled. "Someone in this room is hungry. Let's eat. Then you can show me those drawings."

"And after that?" She gave a wicked grin.

He'd talk to her. Depending on her reaction, either they'd end up in bed or not. He managed a smile that must not have been convincing because she frowned.

"Is anything wrong?"

"Yeah. I'm hungry, too."

The frown faded. "In more ways than one, huh? I get that."

After dinner, they headed into the living room and sat on the couch, where she handed him printouts of the drawings. They looked them over together and she answered his questions. Then she put them into an envelope. "These are yours now."

"I like what you did. When the couch and chair cushions are padded again and all the furniture is re-covered, this place will look great. The bedroom layout will change up that room, too. Will you help me find the right fabric for the furniture in both rooms?"

"You didn't see anything in the books you borrowed?"

"One or two possibilities, but I'm not able to visualize how they'll look. Why don't you choose what you think will work? I'm fairly open, as long as it's not frou-frou."

"And here I was thinking pink satin," she teased. "Of course, I'll help you. We'll go through the books again and I'll order samples to try that will work with the wall colors. Unless you haven't picked that out, either?"

"I need help there, too. What do I owe you for the drawings?"

"I don't feel right about charging you."

"None of that." He set his jaw. "This is business, your livelihood. What would you charge someone you weren't involved with?"

"A while back I said I'd give you a discount, remember?" Even with that, the amount she quoted wasn't cheap. Well worth the cost, though.

"I'm not set up yet to take credit cards," she told him.

"No problem." He wrote her a check.

"Thanks, Kenny. You're such a great guy." She gazed up at him with the big eyes he was a sucker for and he wanted to forget what he needed to tell her and head for the bedroom. But she ought to know.

As she leaned up to kiss him, he stopped her. Confusion etched tiny lines between her brows. "You don't want sex tonight?"

"Oh, I want it. But not until I talk to you."

"You mentioned that this morning." She gave him a leery look. "That somber face worries me. Is there a problem?"

"You tell me." He jumped straight to the bottom line. "I'm going on a date."

By her raised eyebrows, she'd been caught off-guard. "Already?"

"You knew it was going to happen."

She glanced at her wool pants and smoothed them over her thighs as if deep in thought. "Right, but I wasn't expecting it quite so soon. I'm glad you told me. It's no big deal, really."

Because she wouldn't quite meet his eyes, he knew it bothered her. "FYI, *she* asked *me* out."

"I don't blame her. You're a good-looking man. Did you meet her through a dating site?"

He shook his head. "Believe it or not, it was at Gifford's. I stopped there after I left Peter's Wednesday afternoon to order trim for the kitchen and the upstairs master bath. I won't need either for a few days, but it's always good to order in advance."

"Does she work there?"

"Margot. That's her name. No, she teaches kindergarten. She was looking for knobs for her kitchen cabinets, saw me, and asked for help. We got to talking, she did a little flirting, then she asked me out. In case you're wondering, no, I didn't flirt back."

"*Pfft,* who you flirt with is none of my business." She flipped her hand in an I-don't-care gesture. "If she teaches kindergarten, she must like kids. When is this big date?"

"Nothing big about it, just a get-acquainted chat over a casual meal at the Come on In. She's meeting me there tomorrow night." Silence, and more smoothing of pants. Not a good sign. "There's nothing between her and me at all, Rose. Heck, I just met the woman."

"You don't have to make excuses. It's really none of my business who you date or when. This is what you want, and I support you." The assurances didn't fool him. She wasn't happy about this. He didn't feel so great, either. "Where does this leave us?"

"Back to how we were pre-sex."

"I thought… We agreed to have sex until I got serious with someone."

"I've changed my mind."

Oh, man, he didn't want to stop what they both enjoyed. "Starting when?"

"Right now."

Wanting each other but keeping a distance? He dreaded that. "That's not going to be easy."

"It will be once I move and we rarely see each other."

The thought wrenched something in his chest. "You'll still help me with fabrics and colors, though?" he asked.

"Of course. You're my first real client."

She turned her head away, but not before he saw the sheen of moisture in her eyes. Or at least imagined it. Now he felt worse than before. When they'd decided to be FWB, she'd seemed okay about him dating to find someone to build a family with.

He knew now she wasn't, not anymore.

"Please, don't cry," he said.

She swiped her eyes and turned toward him. "Don't flatter yourself. FYI, I had something in my eye. I think it's gone now."

She yawned and stood up. "The last day of the sale at Panache is tomorrow, and business should be brisk. I need a decent night's sleep. Thanks for dinner."

"Back at ya for the drawings. Let me know when you have time to look at fabrics."

"I will." There was no goodnight kiss or anything but more silence.

Hating to watch her go like that, but seeing no way to fix it, he walked her to the door and stayed in the threshold until she drove away.

* * *

HER MIND in turmoil and in no mood to go back to the torn-up house, Rose drove straight to Melissa Ann's to pick up a treat or three. Tears dammed up behind her eyes, but she refused to let them out. Kenny's unexpected news rattled her but shouldn't have. Not that long ago, she'd given him the okay to date and had meant it at the time. Mainly because the whole idea had seemed so far away and unlikely.

Hadn't Ragan and Pressley warned her? The idea of him actually having a date… She hated the thought, was nowhere ready to give up what they shared.

If only she hadn't fallen for him. Should've known better than to get involved in the first place. Damn her hungry body for convincing her she could handle a FWB relationship.

Everything in the bakery tempted her, and she left with three boxes—one with assorted cookies, another with chocolate eclairs, and a third with buttery cinnamon rolls, much-needed treats to bolster her spirits. Then she headed straight to Vi and Blake's. She wanted, needed to talk with her sister. Not for advice, just to let out her feelings with someone who loved her. Also to share the good news about the permanent job at Thompson's.

The newlyweds lived in Blake's beautiful home in an upscale area on the east side of town, complete with a view of the ocean from a gorgeous wood deck. Treats in hand, she headed to the front door. No one answered. Out on a Thursday night? Well, shoot.

Back in the car with the engine running and the heat on high, she phoned Pressley, then Ragan. Neither one answered. Rose heaved a sigh. On her own for the rest of the evening. She wasn't about to head back to the mess at Peter's house yet.

Where to go now? Some place where she could forget her troubles for a while. The Majestic Theater, a dine-in movie house about ten miles west of downtown, was exactly what she needed. Having eaten, she'd skip the food, sneak in a cookie or two, and lose herself in a movie. Any one would do. There were six separate theaters to choose from.

As luck had it, "The Fall Guy" was playing in one of them. It'd come out the previous year to good reviews, but she hadn't seen it. After buying herself a ticket online, she parked in the lot and sent a group text to her sister and besties. *Good news: I'm hired full-time at Thompson's starting when I finish the quarter! Bad news: FWB is over.*

She sent a similar message to Gran without the bad news. Then she silenced her phone, bought a bag of movie popcorn to go with the cookies stashed in her purse—a sweet and salty munch fest—and enjoyed the movie without a thought of anyone or anything else. Mission accomplished, and a stomach way too full of popcorn and cookies.

Determined to think about the movie, the upcoming move into the apartment, and the full-time job for the rest of the evening, she left her phone off. Before heading for Peter's, she stopped at the bank and deposited Kenny's check, pleased with her growing bank balance. She refused to think about the date he was going on tomorrow evening or let her unhappiness about that get the best of her.

In other words, she thought about it a lot. No more Kenny to share her days with. No more holding each other and him listening to her and cheering her on, no more wonderful sex. All of that was behind her now. She had no illusions of keeping their friendship alive, especially if this thing with Margot got serious. Whether or not she was the one for him, sooner or later he was bound to meet the right someone and settle down.

He deserved his happily-ever-after. She totally understood that.

So why did it hurt so much?

CHAPTER 26

Friday, Rose showed up early at Panache, same as the assistant manager, Electra, and Penny. Despite the sale ending the previous Sunday, new customers attracted by the event came back, which was great. The ton of sales she'd made both during the sale and today meant an even fatter paycheck ahead.

Another plus: she didn't have a second to angst about Kenny's date tonight. The mere thought of him with another woman made her want to kick something, but that'd hurt her toes, and the ankle boots she was wearing were uncomfortable enough without making things worse.

Never mind, she had her own plans tonight—getting together with Vi, Pressley, and Ragan. They'd read her text and wanted more info. As wearing as the day was, Rose looked forward to hanging out with them later. Their love and support meant a great deal to her, and the conversation ought to keep her mind off Kenny. They planned to meet at the Bluebird, about five miles west of the ferry terminal, and famous for its beef stew and homemade bread. Rose hadn't been there in a long time.

Due to straightening the mess left after the hordes cleared out of the store, she left later than planned. She texted to let her dinner companions know she'd be late and arrived a good fifteen minutes after the scheduled time. Vi had reserved a table, and she and the others were sipping drinks and enjoying themselves. Eager to relax and join the fun, Rose hurried toward them.

It wasn't long before her own cocktail arrived. Aah. "Panache was a zoo," she told them. "It feels so good to sit down with you all and sip my Sazerac. I'm looking forward to a salad, the stew, and that yummy bread slathered with butter." She rubbed her stomach.

"Aren't we all," Ragan said. "Congrats on the full-time job. "Didn't Pressley and I say it was yours if you wanted it?"

"Your first full-time job." Vi beamed at her. "I'm proud of you."

"I'm proud of me too, and I really appreciate your support."

"That's the good news," Vi said. "Tell us about Kenny."

"And the end of the FWB deal," Pressley said, frowning. "You seemed so happy about that. What went wrong?"

One look at the sympathetic faces of the three women, and Rose's spirits plummeted. The tears she'd assured herself were over and done with gathered behind her eyes. She blinked them away. "I don't want to bore you with the whole story. In a nutshell, he has a date tonight."

"You're crying," Vi noted.

Rose shook her head. "No, I'm not."

"You are, too. It's okay. We've all seen it before and done it ourselves."

Hard to put anything past her sister. "Maybe I don't want to do it right now." Rose blinked hard and dabbed away the last hint of moisture. "I'm good now."

"You knew this was going to happen," Ragan commented. Vi and Pressley nodded. "You said you were fine with it."

"I thought I was. As it turns out, I was mistaken."

Vi studied her. "I can't tell if you're sad or mad."

"Both. Sad because I'm going to miss Kenny. Being with him is fun and interesting, and yes, the sex is so good. Mad at myself for not thinking things through and for agreeing to the FWB thing in the first place." She thought a minute. "I'm not mad about that." It'd been too wonderful to regret. "What really bothers me is the thought of him with another woman." Grr. She glanced from Pressley to Ragan. "You warned me about the fall out, but I didn't listen. I should've."

"Are you in love with him?" Vi asked.

They leaned forward with intent expressions that made her feel like a woman under investigation for a crime. Share the truth or not? Rose swallowed and let it out. "Unfortunately, yes, and don't any of you tell another soul." She sighed. "It was fun while it lasted."

"I'm sorry you're going through this," Vi said. "What's your next move?"

Of course, she wanted to know. She always had thought ahead and strategized how to proceed. "I have no idea—I just found out about the date last night. The only thing I'm reasonably sure of is that once I move into my apartment, and as soon as I finish helping him with his place, I probably won't see him again."

This time, she didn't fight the tears.

* * *

THAT SAME NIGHT on the south side of town, Kenny met Margot in front of the Come on In. It was a cold, dark evening, the wind brisk and biting. Instead of hurrying inside to get warm, Margot insisted on a selfie of the two of them standing under the funky, backlit Come on In sign in front of the diner. Go figure. They sat down in a booth and ordered drinks and dinner.

The evening started off well enough. Outgoing and talkative, Margot was involved with something called clog dancing, which she explained as a mixture of Irish, tap, and hip hop. She'd met her ex-boyfriend, whose name was Claude, there. Having never heard of that kind of dancing, Kenny enjoyed learning about it. At least at first. Barely pausing to eat, she went on and on about the weekly dances and competitions she and Claude had once signed up for.

After a trip to the bathroom, she returned to her seat. She showed no interest in Kenny or any of the comments he managed to squeeze in, wanted only to reminisce about the good times with Claude, who she clearly still had a thing for.

So different from Rose, stopping herself when she thought she was talking too much and caring about what he had to say. Listening to her had never bored him.

Margot bored him silly. She didn't seem to notice his disinterest, or maybe she didn't care. He gave off plenty of signals—yawns, stretches, and frequent glances at his watch. She paused to fiddle with her phone. "What are you doing?" he asked.

"Nothing. Just sending a photo."

"What photo?"

"The one I took of us."

"What? Why would you do that?"

"Since you asked, I want to make him jealous. You're good looking. He needs to know that guys like you are attracted to me, and that I'm a catch." Not a shred of embarrassment from her.

"That's whack. Erase it from your phone."

"What good would that do, when I sent it?"

He snorted. "I don't want him or anybody else getting the wrong idea." With a no-nonsense expression, he nodded his chin at her phone. "Erase it. Now."

"Geez," she grumbled. "Okay."

"Tell him what you did."

"I'm not going to do that."

"No problem, I'll find him on social media and tell him myself." Finally, a reaction. She looked appalled.

He stood.

"Where are you going?" she asked, all confused.

"I can't say this has been fun. It hasn't. You used me to make your ex jealous. Don't expect me to pay for the meal. That's on you. I'm outta here."

For the first time that evening, she was speechless. He was surprised at himself for leaving her with the check, but he was nobody's fool. Without a backward glance, he stalked out.

Wait'll Rose heard about this. He wanted to tell her, but his gut told him she wouldn't want to know, at least not now. She'd had a busy day at Panache. When he got home, he texted Buddha.

Had a date tonight that sucked.

He didn't hear back and didn't expect to, just needed to tell his buddy.

Saturday, he woke feeling out of sorts. It sucked to mess up what he had with Rose only to be used by Margot. Maybe when he shared the details with her, she'd want to continue their relationship. He had his doubts about that. In no mood to make his own breakfast and preferring to eat in a crowd of strangers, which was better than his own lousy company, he climbed into the truck. He ate at Hastings, a popular local chain with decent coffee and breakfasts. When he finished the meal, he headed toward home, his thoughts on Rose. He really wanted to talk to her. Too bad she was at Panache today. He didn't realize where he was going until he pulled into the parking area at the boutique.

CHAPTER 27

Compared with the previous day's sales at Panache, business was slow Saturday. So slow that Electra went home and Penny took her lunch break early. As soon as she returned to the shop, Rose would take her turn. Not that she had any place special in mind. Whatever she ended up eating, she'd pick up enough for leftovers. She was refolding tops and jeans when the door jingled, signaling a customer.

But the man who stepped inside was no customer. Kenny. Hating the way her heartbeat hitched up, she reorganized the tops she'd just folded and sorted by size.

"Hey," he called out to her. "Slow day?"

"Super slow."

Like a moth drawn to the light on a dark night, she left the table and headed straight toward him. She wanted details about his date the previous night. As long as it wasn't something about how they'd gotten along really well and had scheduled another date. "What are you doing here?"

He scratched his head as if he had no idea, then scrubbed his hand through his hair. "My date was a bomb."

Funny how that cheered her up. "Must've been really bad if you drove over here to tell me. It's a good thing there aren't any customers around."

"Yeah, I thought about that. Don't worry, if anyone comes, I'll pretend to be looking for something."

"But not for Margot?"

He looked as if he'd swallowed a fly. "Hell, no. Do you have time to talk? I really want to tell you about it."

Her mind conjured up possibilities—Margot had jumped his bones and the sex had been awful. She smelled, had bad breath, was too tense for conversation. Rose barely restrained her over-the-top curiosity. "I have things to do, but I guess I can spare five minutes."

"I'll talk fast. It was weird from the beginning. She started off insisting on a selfie of us standing under the Come on In sign, like we were a couple." He grimaced. "First, she took a selfie of me and her in front of the diner sign. I thought that was weird. Then over dinner, she told me about clogging, a dance thing she's into, courtesy of her ex. She never shut her mouth about that and him. It was like I wasn't even there. Then, right in front of me, she sent the photo she'd taken to her ex. Guess why—she thought if he saw the snapshot of her with me, he'd realize she was a catch." He rolled his eyes. "A catch that bored me silly."

Rose's jaw dropped. "No way. I'm shocked that any woman would stoop so low, let alone admit it."

"It was pretty awful. Can you believe that?"

He looked so alarmed that Rose surprised herself and laughed. "Of all the things I imagined about your date, that never entered my mind."

His lips twitched, and he smiled. "It wasn't funny last

night. At least she gave me an excuse to leave." He lowered his voice. "I told her I didn't like being used and made her pay for the meal. And I made sure she deleted that selfie."

Secretly pleased about the miserable date, Rose shook her head. "What a sad story."

"One for the books, that's for sure. A waste of an evening I could've spent with you if it hadn't been on the last day of the sale. I know how tiring that must've been. Do you want to have dinner tonight? We'll go someplace nice to celebrate your full-time job."

She really wanted that but in the interest of self-preservation—starting up again, then stopping wouldn't do her or Kenny any good—she shook her head. "I don't think so. Pretty soon, you'll meet someone else to take out and then someone else, until you find the woman you're looking for. I'd rather not fall back into what we were doing only to stop again."

He seemed disappointed. "It was worth a try asking. Can I have one last hug?"

"Now?" She glanced around.

"We're the only ones here. If you're worried someone will see us through the window, we could go into the back room, if there is one."

She didn't need a hug, but oh, how she wanted the feel of his arms around her one final time. "Follow me," she said, and led him past the shelves and racks where inventory was stored, then through a hallway to the break room. "In there."

Without a word, he pulled her close, breasts to chest, hips to groin. Warm and safe and wonderful. She let out a sigh of relief. Against her better judgment, she clung to him way too long. He was aroused—she felt it. So was she, but she couldn't let anything more than the hug happen. Unable to help herself, she let go of him and cupped his handsome face in her hands. She kissed him with passion and melancholy.

The long look they shared as they parted hurt because it was the last.

"I won't be seeing you again?" he asked as she escorted him toward the door of the shop.

"Maybe at Peter's, and of course to show you my ideas for fabrics and colors in the rooms I sketched. We end there. It's only fair to you and to me." Darned if her eyes didn't fill.

He swallowed hard, almost as if he were battling his own tears. "We should finish up at Peter's by the end of next week. Right on time."

"Good—you'll get that bonus. Text me when the kitchen is done, and I'll make sure the movers come back to return the fridge and other appliances to the kitchen."

"No need. We'll take care of that."

"It's already paid for. Before I forget, next Friday the consignment company will pick up the last of the furniture. I'm stowing the office table and chairs and the copy machine in the closet of my apartment. Would you believe the table folds up? I'll come over after I finish at Panache that evening to get the last of my stuff and take a look around."

"But you aren't able to get into the apartment yet. If you need a place to stay Friday night, you're welcome at my place. I have plenty of room, and I swear, I won't lay a hand on you."

Being alone with him was more trouble waiting to happen. "I can't do that, Kenny. I'll be at Vi and Blake's."

He nodded. "Peter's house will need a thorough cleaning."

"I don't have to worry about that. He scheduled a staging company to clean and make the place look pretty. He's going to make a mint."

Overcome with sadness, she couldn't and didn't want to say goodbye. Her heart felt as if it cracked. "Take care, Kenny."

"You, too," he said, his voice gruff with feeling.

Watching him trudge across the parking lot to his truck, she sniffled and fished in her purse for a tissue. Not long after he left, Penny returned from lunch. Having lost her appetite, Rose skipped eating and wandered aimlessly around the wintry neighborhood, feeling cold inside and out.

* * *

A FEW WEEKS LATER, Kenny met Buddha at the bowling alley. He bowled a lousy game. Instead of gloating, Buddha looked worried. "You're not your usual self," he said as they ate hotdogs and chips and sipped beer. "Let me guess—things didn't go well with the woman you met for coffee the other day."

Kenny shrugged. "It didn't go at all. I canceled."

"What? I thought you were gung-ho about meeting the right woman for you."

"I was, but that first dinner out and my last two coffee dates sucked. Why waste another hour of my time? Besides, I started on a new project and my plate is full."

"You're busy, I get that. But if you really want to meet someone, you gotta get out there. My gut tells me Rose has something to do with your hesitation." Hard to argue with that. "You have to forget her, man. Have you seen her lately?"

"When we finished the renovations last week, I did a final walk-through with her."

"And?"

"She was friendly enough." Like they were no more than

casual acquaintances. "She sent Peter a bunch of photos. I finished within his six-to-eight-week timeline, and he paid me the bonus he promised."

"Nice. Are you planning on seeing Rose again?"

Not the way Kenny wanted to. "We're meeting at Thompson's next week for a final okay on the fabrics and wall colors she picked out, but that's a business thing. Last weekend, she moved into her new place. Her brother-in-law, Blake, says she's throwing a party soon to show it to her friends and family, but I don't know when. I doubt she wants me to come. I'll find out when I see her at Thompson's."

"Anything after that?"

"Nada."

"Good. Maybe you'll finally be able to forget her."

"Will I?" Kenny blew out a heavy breath. "I miss her, man."

"You're in love with her. I knew that would happen."

Kenny didn't deny it. "I didn't plan to feel this way."

"Love happens when it happens. I haven't seen you this miserable since you called it quits with Crystal."

This was far worse.

"What are you going to do about it?"

"Like you said, get over her. Better that way. I'm pretty sure my feelings are stronger than hers. Then there's the kid thing. She doesn't want them, and you know how I feel about that. It's a deal-breaker."

"So you keep saying. How do you expect to find the woman you're looking for without getting out there and dating? You can't let a few bum dates stop you."

"So far, none of the women I've shared coffee with have interested me. And don't tell me I'm getting in my own way because of my feelings for Rose. I'm aware of that. She's the one I want. I wish to hell I knew how to stop."

"You sound like a broken record," Buddha muttered. "Here's my $.50. Unless you change your mind about kids, and that's doubtful, put yourself out there, forget Rose, or at least fake it till you believe it, and give dating your all. If you don't, nothing will change."

CHAPTER 28

The afternoon before the last day of her internship and a week before the official last day of the quarter, after working daily on her final paper in the peace and quiet of her new apartment, Rose finished the rough draft. And the paper wasn't due for another few days. Oh, that felt good. Next on the list, prepare to pass the NCIDQ exam in April. She'd been studying for it along with the rest of the class and was confident that if she kept at it, she'd pass. Meanwhile, she'd be happily working full-time at Thompson's, the job of her dreams.

As thrilled as she was about the way her career was going, something was missing from her life. Kenny. She hadn't seen him in weeks. They'd scheduled an appointment at Thompson's for the following afternoon. There was so much she wanted to know. Had he met someone he could see settling down with? The very thought made her stomach clench. She caught herself rubbing her arms as if she were cold, when the cozy apartment was warm.

"Stop it," she ordered out loud. When that didn't work, she phoned Vi.

"Hey, you," her sister answered with a smile in her voice.

"Hi. I finished the draft of my final paper ahead of time. I still have to read through it tonight, but it'll be ready to turn in Friday. I'm going to leave it with Tommie's secretary on my way to Panache."

"You're amazing!"

Sharing with her sister, who really cared, felt good. But not as good as sharing with Kenny. "I still need to add photos and a few drawings, but those things shouldn't take long."

"I have no doubt your teacher will love it. When do you start full-time at Thompson's?"

"They're giving me ten days off after I graduate. So nice of them. My start day is March 17, St. Pat's Day. This Friday is my last day at Panache."

"A nice breather from your hectic life. I'll bet you're glad about that, and especially about leaving Panache."

"Working there wasn't so bad, but it'll be much more fun shopping there instead."

"Look how much you've accomplished in the last almost three months. You're managing a budget and living in your own apartment, which I can't wait to see at your housewarming party. Not only that, you're graduating from school with a great job and a fabulous future ahead. Everything in your life is good, so where's that enthusiasm?"

"I've been up late working on this paper and I'm tired," Rose said. Which was the truth but not the whole story. She wouldn't mention Kenny. "You don't have to wait that long to see the apartment. Come over any time."

"I might take you up on that. Tell me the real reason you're less than thrilled about your life. Wait, let me guess. You miss Kenny."

"So much." It was a good thing Vi couldn't see the misery on her face. At least she wasn't crying.

"You haven't mentioned him in a while, but I had a hunch. Have you talked to him at all?"

"No, but he's meeting me at Thompson's tomorrow. I'm worried I won't be able to hold myself together. I don't want to look like a fool. I haven't felt this anxious since Peter left. What's wrong with me?"

"You love him."

That said it all. "If I could stop, believe me, I would. I don't know what to do about it. I'm not going to tell him, that's for sure."

"I understand completely. I was scared to tell Blake how I felt and didn't for a while. All I knew was, when I was with him I felt whole. When I didn't think he'd be around anymore, my heart ached for him and life seemed emptier. Is that how you feel?"

"Pretty much."

"You have to tell him, Rose. Otherwise, he'll move on." While Rose thought about that, Vi added, "Believe me, telling him is worth the risk of looking foolish. For what it's worth, I can't imagine Kenny ever seeing you that way."

She was probably right about that, yet there was no way to be sure. "But we have different views of the future that make us incompatible. For all I know, he's met someone who wants the same things he does."

"You mean children. That's a tough one I don't have an

answer for. Know that I'll be thinking of you tomorrow. Call me at work if you need to."

AFTER A FITFUL NIGHT—BE honest with Kenny or pretend everything was fine?—Rose decided not to give herself away when she saw him at Thompson's. Not that she would at work, but afterward… Regardless what Vi said, admitting her feelings when he could very well be falling for someone else was too dangerous. Then there was the issue about kids.

Still, wanting to look her best for him, she dressed carefully. And threw herself into helping customers. The day passed fairly quickly, and soon it was time for him to arrive.

He'd shown up late for his first visit to Thompson's and might again, if he came at all. Having not seen him since he'd stopped in at Panache weeks earlier, she wasn't sure he would. A ball of nerves, she checked her watch more than once. When he finally entered the store within minutes of his appointment time, she heaved a sigh of relief. Her hungry eyes devoured the sight of him. He was dressed in a Henley shirt and jeans that emphasized his muscled body. So handsome.

"It's good to see you," he said, friendly but not overly so, when she approached him.

Must've met someone. Her heart sank. "You, too," she said brightly. "It's been awhile. How are things?"

"Not bad. Last week, I started a new renovation project not far from Peter's house."

She was pretty sure she knew whose home he was working on. "The Lessigs hired you. I'm glad they took my advice and contacted you."

"That's how they heard about me? I didn't realize." For a fleeting moment, his eyes warmed the way they once had. "Thanks for the recommendation."

It was obvious that the warmth stemmed from gratitude, not feelings for her. She forced a smile. "You're welcome. I hope you'll do the same for me when you hear of someone wanting design help."

"That's a good idea. We should trade cards. I don't have any with me, but I'll get some to you."

"Remind me to give you some of mine before you leave today."

"Okay. So this is your last day as an intern."

"Yes, and it went by so fast. I'll show you the fabrics I picked out for you. If you like what you see, we'll look at wall colors that could complement them."

Working with him was a joy. He was really interested in what she had to say and even cracked a few jokes, almost as if they'd never been apart. But they weren't seeing each other anymore, and she'd best remember that. "How's the dating going?" she asked, catching her breath. He made a so-so gesture with his hand, and she could breathe again. "That's too bad."

No reaction. "How's the apartment?"

"I love living there. If you want to see it, I'm throwing a celebration/housewarming party the day after I graduate, which is a week from tomorrow! Pretty exciting. The party is the following night, which happens to be a Saturday."

He didn't comment on that. "No more weekends at Panache?"

"Tomorrow's my last day there. Anyway, if you want to

stop by and see the apartment during the party…" She let the words trail off.

"Appreciate the invite. I'm not sure I can make it."

He must have plans, possibly a date. Keeping her expression carefully blank, she nodded.

When he left, the world seemed dull and colorless, and her heart? Well, it ached.

What a foolish, foolish woman she was, falling for him.

CHAPTER 29

Kenny left Thompson's in low spirits. He'd looked forward to seeing Rose today. Despite trying hard to forget her, he hadn't and wondered if he ever would. As always, she looked great and from what he could tell, she seemed happy enough. She'd been friendly, but without the warmth that meant so much. Clearly, she'd moved on.

"What did you expect, fool?" he muttered in the car. Should've taken her at her word when she'd said she didn't want love, canceled today's meeting, and managed the fabric and paint on his own.

In need of something to eat, he ordered pizza to go from Pinole's. On the way there, he stopped at Collingwood's grocery and bought chocolate chip cookies and a six-pack of beer. His pizza wasn't ready. While he waited at a table, an attractive female about his age wandered toward him. She gave a flirty smile. In no mood to smile back, he pulled out his phone and checked for messages. The woman sat down at the same table. "Is this seat taken?"

Buddha's advice echoed in his head. *Put yourself out there, forget Rose or at least pretend to, and give dating your all.* "Take it," he said, stood, and sauntered toward the order counter.

As usual, Maria was there. "Where's your beautiful friend, Rose?" she asked as she boxed his pie.

"I have no idea."

She gave him a long, level look. "If you're not careful, you'll lose her."

He already had.

For the next week, he did everything he could to forget her. He had coffee with two different women. Both were friendly and the dates went fairly well, but they weren't Rose, and he couldn't summon much interest. The rest of the time, he kept his head down and worked until he was too tired to think. The fabric arrived and he carted his living room furniture to a shop that specialized in repadding cushions and recovering sofas and chairs. A process that would take weeks. While he waited for that, he stayed up late painting the walls and ceilings.

Sleep came in fits and starts. Late at night, he lay in bed pining for Rose when he knew better. Too bad they wanted different things. She'd made her peace with that and moved on; so should he.

An impossible task.

Try as he might, he couldn't see a way to breach the gap between them.

* * *

As SCHOOL WOUND TO A CLOSE, Rose found herself thinking about the future. Not her career, which was on the right track. Relationships, specifically with Kenny. Did she really want to spend the rest of her life without him? She stopped herself right there. A walk in the fresh air would clear the clutter from her mind and help her gain perspective. She hadn't explored her new neighborhood, and this was the perfect time.

She set out down the block. It was late morning and partly sunny in the quiet neighborhood. Despite the cold air, spring was on the horizon. A few hardy birds called out, and she saw a robin building a nest. Flower shoots poked out of the ground, and scattered crocuses looked ready to bloom.

She didn't want to lose Kenny but it was bound to happen if she didn't change her mind about children. The trouble was, she'd never wanted to be a mother. Who knew why.

Suddenly, she heard the desolate sobs of a young child. Not far from where she was, a little girl who looked to be three or four stood on the sidewalk all alone, looking lost and scared. No coat, no gloves, and no sign of an adult or any kids around. Having been there herself, heart constricting, she approached. "Are you okay?" she asked in a crooning voice she didn't recognize.

The little girl looked at her. "I w-want my mommy."

"What's your name?"

"B-Becky."

"I'm Rose. You look cold. Is it okay if I put my scarf around you?" She took off her wool scarf, which was big enough to wrap around the small girl. Becky's nose was running, and Rose fished in her pocket for a tissue to wipe her nose. "Where do you live, sweetie?'

"On Balter Street."

A street she hadn't heard of. "Is it far from here?"

"I don't know." The wailing increased.

Having no idea what to do, Rose hunkered down and pulled her into a hug. The little body trembled, but she burrowed in close. Warmth filled her heart. "We'll find the house," she said.

Becky sniffled and nodded. Her trust felt good. Now what? "What's your last name, Becky?"

"Hawington."

"Harrington?"

"Uh-huh."

"That's good to know." Becky had stopped crying. Rose reached for her hand and pointed to a house down the block, the only one with a car in the driveway. Maybe someone who knew the girl was home and knew where Balter Street was. "Shall we go and look there?" Clutching hold of her hand, the girl nodded.

She was about to ring the doorbell when a youngish woman rushed toward them. "Becky!" she called out.

"Mama." They reached each other in record time.

The woman scooped up her daughter and nuzzled her. "I was so worried," she told Rose. "We were visiting a friend the next block up. The front door didn't close, and suddenly she was gone. Thank you—I don't know your name."

"I'm Rose."

"April. Where did you find her?"

Rose pointed behind her. "I was taking a walk and heard her crying. We were about to look for you."

"Thank you for helping her, Rose, and for wrapping her up in that scarf. I'm so grateful." The woman handed it back to her and made room in her parka for her daughter.

"I'm happy I could help." Rose meant that and was proud of herself.

"What do you say to Rose?" April prodded.

"Tank you," came the little voice.

Apparently, she hadn't mastered the 'th' sound. So cute. "You're welcome, Becky."

Kids weren't so bad, she mused as she resumed her walk and went back to puzzling over why she'd never wanted one. Now, she realized she wouldn't mind having a little Becky of her own. A thought that astounded her.

On the heels of the thought, she suddenly understood why she'd never wanted kids: she was wary of perpetuating the same cycle of neglect as Angela and ruining the life of an innocent child who depended on her.

How had she not figured this out a long time ago? Because she'd never had reason to think about children, and *that* was because she'd never truly loved a man enough to contemplate having one of her own. Until Kenny.

Unlike her own father, who was every bit as neglectful as Angela, Kenny would make a great dad. She was sure of that, but kids needed a competent mom, too. Changing her mind about children wasn't enough. Angela had been a terrible role model. Was she capable of doing a better job? The thought of failing terrified her, but now… Having successfully rescued and calmed Becky, she might.

She wanted to run her new understanding past Vi and her best friends. When classes ended and she'd turned in her final paper and was free of commitments until her party the coming Saturday, she invited them over to show them her apartment in advance of the open house and get their opinions about the mothering thing.

Like her, they loved the little place she now called home. While they sipped wine—cider for Vi—Rose shared her newfound understanding and fears with them. "Knowing all that, do you think I could be a decent mom?"

The three of them exchanged looks, then chimed in.

"I never understood why you didn't want to have kids," Vi said, running her palm over her as yet small baby bump. "Now I get it."

"Not every woman wants children, and I figured you were one of them." Ragan shrugged. "This changes everything."

"Sure does," Pressley agreed. "What inspired this new outlook?"

"My feelings for Kenny. I love him. Vi knows that, but the two of you don't."

"We had a strong hunch," Ragan said. "You seem iffy, though. I'm not sure about what."

Rose caught herself gnawing on her pinkie nail, and put her hand in her lap. "The thing is, I don't know if he still wants me."

"Then find out," Pressley advised.

Vi leaned forward. "I have to ask—what if he's moved on? If he met someone else, would you still want a child?"

The thought of life without him hurt terribly. "Right now, all I can think about is being with him and having our baby."

"Kids are a huge responsibility," Ragan added. "Once you have one, you can't send it back. When you talk to Kenny, you owe it to him to share your concerns."

Scary, but necessary. Rose swallowed. "I will."

Her sister raised an eyebrow. "When and what will you say to him?"

Rose hadn't thought that far ahead. If he showed up at her party, she'd let him know she wanted to talk. But she doubted he'd show up. Otherwise..."Soon. I'm not sure what I'll say yet, but—"

Raising her index finger, Ragan interrupted. "Adding to what Vi said, what if you bare your heart to him and *then* find out he's moved on? You've always worried about people seeing you as foolish."

"I'm working on that," Rose said, although the fear was still with her. "For a fresh chance with Kenny, I'm willing to risk it."

CHAPTER 30

The family—Gran, Malcom, Vi, and Blake—celebrated Rose's graduation with dinner at Sea Captain's Café. The restaurant was a favorite of the grandparents. As soon as they sat down at Gran and Malcom's usual table with its panoramic view of the ocean, Gran handed her an envelope. Inside was a generous check. "This is from the four of us. We're all so proud of you."

"You're off to a great start of a wonderful career," Malcom added.

Rose beamed. "That means a lot to me. I love you all."

"Did you call your mom and tell her you graduated?" Gran wanted to know.

Rose nodded. It'd been a short conversation, as Angela had been getting ready to go out with her latest boyfriend. "She's happy for me and sends her love. I can't wait to show you my cute apartment!" She had everything she wanted except Kenny, but she wasn't going to let that get in the way of the family's festivities. "Of course, I showed it to Vi a few days ago."

"Big sister privileges," Vi said. "But you'll all see it tomorrow night."

"We're looking forward to that, aren't we Malcom?" Gran said.

"Very much so. You've grown up and quite nicely since I first met you."

A real compliment coming from the extremely successful former business magnate. "Is there anyone special coming?" Gran asked.

"You mean a man I'm interested in? How did you know I've met someone?"

"I didn't, but now I'm glad I asked. Who is this mystery man?"

To tell, or not to tell… Rose glanced at Vi, who nodded at her to answer the question. "His name is Kenny Martin."

Gran's eyes widened. "The man who built your shed, Blake. How did you meet him, Rose?"

"He's the contractor Peter hired."

Blake nodded. "I recommended him. That was before I knew what Peter had in mind."

"And you've been hiding this relationship with Kenny?" Gran looked hurt.

Instant guilt. "I should've said something. He's a busy man, and I'm not sure he'll be at the housewarming."

"He'd better be," her grandmother muttered.

Rose gave the woman a stern look. "Please, stay out of my business."

"All right. Should we bring anything when we come?"

"Just yourselves. I have a ton of food, several bottles of wine, and enough pop to swim in."

When the meal ended and Rose went home, she cleaned

the apartment top to bottom. She spent a good part of Saturday getting ready for the housewarming and thinking about Kenny. "I shouldn't get my hopes up that he'll come," she told herself out loud.

If he didn't, she'd go to him.

* * *

BEFORE DAWN the Saturday of Rose's housewarming party, Kenny jerked awake from a dreamless sleep, the first he'd had in a long time. While he was in la-la land, the answer he'd been looking for to resuscitate his relationship with Rose had come to him. Amazing.

Attempting to follow Buddha's advice had been a complete failure. What stuck with him was Maria's warning to be careful or he'd lose her. He'd been living with the misery of already having done that, but what if there was still a chance? With the idea that his brain had worked out, there might be.

Unless she was through with him no matter what.

For a moment, the world darkened. But no, he wouldn't let that stop him from trying. When he'd last seen her at Thompson's, she'd left him with mixed messages: goodbye for good, yet also inviting him to the housewarming.

He hadn't planned to show up but changed his mind. For much of the day, he worked on a hand-crafted housewarming gift for her and thought about the evening ahead.

Impossible to talk privately during a party. He'd approach her and ask to talk to her later, when they could be alone.

Finishing his gift took a while, and he showed up late at the party. She'd said the apartment was small, and it was. The dozen or so people milling around almost filled the living room. He didn't see her but caught sight of his mom, which surprised him. Rose hadn't mentioned inviting her.

"What are you doing here?" he asked when she reached him.

"I have the same question for you. When I was at Panache last week, I found out it was Rose's last day. I'm sure going to miss her next time I shop there. I can't not go back—I've had so many compliments on the dress she helped me pick out. Anyway, we got talking. She told me about graduating with a degree in interior design and about this apartment. She's an awesome woman. She invited me to the housewarming. It's a cute place. That's my story. What's yours?"

He skirted the question. "She invited me, too. I need something to drink."

"Over there on the side table," she said, gesturing toward it. "You came so late," she added as he filled a wine glass. "Lots of people have left." She eyed the brown paper bag in his hand. "What's that?"

"A housewarming gift I made for Rose. Where is she?"

"I'm not sure, but in a place this small, finding her shouldn't be too hard. What did you make her?"

"You'll have to wait and see,"

CHAPTER 31

Doing her best to play the perfect hostess, Rose refilled a tray of appetizers. The party was winding down, with only a handful of family and friends left. Still no sign of Kenny. Oh, well. She'd assumed he wasn't coming, but what a let-down. Determined to stay cheerful, she carried the tray into the living room.

Her eyes gravitated to the man she so wanted to see. Kenny.

He was all dressed up in a pressed burgundy shirt with an open collar, dark pants, and leather lace-ups. He'd helped himself to wine and had the drink in one hand and a brown paper bag in the other and was in conversation with Vi, Blake, Pressley, Ragan, Gran, and Malcom. The entire group of family and friends who knew about her feelings for him. Afraid of what they might be saying, she hurried toward him with the tray in hand.

"You came," she said, smiling. "How about a mini pig-in-a-blanket?"

"Thanks," he said, helping himself. "Apologies for showing up late."

"Don't worry about it. I see you've made friends with my besties and my grandma and her husband."

Also smiling, he nodded. "A nice group of people along with Blake and Vi."

"We like you, too," Gran said.

Save me from the woman's prying ways. "You'll never guess what came in the mail today," she told Kenny. "I already shared this with everyone here. I got the official document proving I'm divorced. Another thing to celebrate tonight."

Kenny raised his glass to that. "Great news."

Brandy wandered over. "Aren't you gonna give her the housewarming gift you brought?"

"Is that what's in the bag?" Rose asked, curious what it could be.

"Why don't you and I talk first." His gaze touched her friends and family, all wide-eyed with interest. "Alone."

That sounded… She wasn't sure what. But he wouldn't want to talk privately unless he had something positive to say. The thought made her slightly breathless, but she managed a calm nod. "All right. Let's go down the hall. I'll give you a tour on the way, although there isn't much to show you. Everybody else, help yourself to food and drink."

Her heart pounding, she showed him the bathroom, bedroom, and the small extra room she used as a makeshift office. She gestured toward that." Let's sit in here. I have things to say to you, too."

He seemed nervous. So was she. "I know you said to wait to open the present till we talk. Can I open it now?"

"When your eyes get all wide and excited, you're not easy to resist. Go ahead." He handed her the bag.

Whatever was in there was oddly shaped. She pulled the item out. Of all the possibilities she'd thought of—vase, book, trivet—she'd never imagined this. "A wooden horseshoe?" she asked, puzzled.

"For good luck in your new place."

"Thanks. I've never seen one like this. It's beautiful, so smooth to the touch."

"I'm glad you like it. The whole time I made it, I thought about you."

"You made this? I'm impressed." She ran her fingers over the satiny wood again. "I'm more interested in finding out what you thought about me while you worked on it."

"I'll tell you in a bit. Ladies first."

Suddenly nervous, she swallowed. "Maybe you should go first."

"Suit yourself. I—" He cleared his throat. "I've missed you."

Aww. She released a sigh. "That's so nice to hear. I've missed you, too. I—"

"I thought I was going first. Okay if I finish?" She nodded and he lifted her hand and kissed it. "I love you, Rose Shafer."

Her heart lifted. "That's so romantic, Kenny, and—"

"I still haven't finished." She shut her mouth, again, and he went on. "I've been driving myself nuts, trying to figure out a way for us to be together when we want different things. I finally figured out how to make this work for us. Now don't fall over in shock, but I've made peace with your decision to not have kids."

She gaped at him. "But you really want them."

"Thought I did. For as long as I can remember, I've wanted

a family of my own. I realize now I don't need children for that. You're my family, Rose, and that's enough."

How she loved him. Her eyes filled.

"Say something," he said.

Despite the tears, she smiled. "So it's my turn now?" He nodded. "First of all, I love you, too."

"Wow." A huge grin lit his face. "Let me get this straight. First, we backed away from each other because we worried one of us loved the other. Then we parted ways for the opposite reason. Now we're cool with loving each other. What a pair we are."

As happy as she was, she eyed him. "Ahem, I also have something important to say."

"Oh." Somber now, he gestured for her to continue.

"Prepare yourself for another opposite. I decided I want to have a baby with you."

His jaw dropped before he shut his mouth. "Did I hear that right?"

She nodded. "But don't get too excited yet." Nervous about what she was about to disclose, she swallowed. "I told you about my mother and my chaotic childhood. I couldn't bear the thought of destroying an innocent child's life the way she did mine and Vi's." Rose bit her thumbnail, then shared her biggest insecurity. "What if I'm as bad a mom as she is?"

He clasped her hands in his and kissed them. "You're too filled with love to be that way."

"But what if I am?"

"I know you won't, but the important thing is how you feel. Would it help if you talked to someone about those fears?"

See a therapist? She'd never considered that. "Maybe."

He shrugged. "It's a suggestion, that's all. We love each other, and we'll work out the rest together." Her heart full, she nodded. His eyes almost twinkled. "Don't I get a thank you for the horseshoe?"

"What do you have in mind?" she teased.

"To start with, a kiss."

"Okay, but that's it. There are people in the other room."

It was a long kiss and not easy to stop. Hand in hand, they headed for the remaining guests.

All of them were gathered in front of the coffee table, their attention on her and Kenny.

Gran's eyes went to their clasped hands. "Looks like it's good news."

Brandy spread her palm across her clavicle and sighed. "Please let that be true."

"The best news ever," Kenny said.

* * *

TEN MONTHS LATER

After taking care of Vi and Blake's adorable daughter, Caro, over the weekend while the parents took a much-deserved break, Rose and Kenny collapsed in front of a crackling fire. Some months earlier, she'd moved into his house. Best decision ever. "Babies sure are a lot of work," she commented.

Kenny shook his head. "And I thought renovations were tough."

"We did it, Kenny. That little sweetie is in my heart forever. I'm so happy I took your advice and had therapy." Thanks to six months of regular counseling, she was confident she wasn't going to repeat Angela's sins, a huge load off her shoulders. "You've been patient with me while I developed the confidence that I can raise a child. I'm finally ready, Kenny. I really want a baby with you."

"You mean it?" he asked, suddenly looking perkier than a moment ago. She nodded. As always, the beautiful smile that bloomed on his face melted her. "When?"

"I'm ready to start trying," she said. "We should probably get married, too."

"Tonight?"

"No, silly. Planning a wedding takes a while. We need at least a month or two lead time. I'll get on that tomorrow."

"Great. I meant make a baby right now."

She yawned. "We're both worn out."

"Trust me, I'll wake you up."

And he did.